YA

CW01082475

LOSING AUSTIN

Michael J. Bowler

Losing Austin

Copyright © 2025 by Michael J. Bowler

All rights reserved.

First Edition: 2025

Paperback ISBN: 979-8-9886110-6-6

Hardback ISBN: 979-8-9886110-7-3

eBook ISBN: 979-8-9886110-8-0

Editor: Loretta Sylvestre

Cover Art: Sanusi Emmanuel

No part of this book may be reproduced, scanned, or distributed in any printed or electronic form without permission. Please do not participate in or encourage piracy of copyrighted materials in violation of the author's rights. Thank you for respecting the hard work of this author.

This is a work of fiction. Names, characters, places, and incidents either are the product of the author's imagination or are used fictitiously, and any resemblance to locales, events, business establishments, or actual persons—living or dead—is entirely coincidental.

 Created with Vellum

Chapter 1

Learn To Control Your Temper, Colton

I made my big brother disappear. Not like a magician makes an elephant disappear, but I *did* drive him away, and he *did* disappear. Did I murder him like everyone thought? No. But since he vanished into thin air, he could have been killed and if he had been, it would've been my fault, but.... I'll explain—even though no one will believe me because, honestly, making elephants disappear is easier to accept than what happened to my brother.

We lived in a town called Mill Valley in Northern California. My expansive, two-story home sat atop Mount Tamalpais, right near the Panoramic Highway that overlooked a mountainside covered with tall, ageless trees and a really amazing view of the Pacific Ocean. At least, that's what my parents kept saying. They took me and Austin on hikes into the woods when we were younger, but by the time I got to middle school, Mom only took Austin because I refused to go. Hiking wasn't my thing, and I didn't give a rip about nature. Seen one tree, seen 'em all.

My house was made of redwood, with tons of windows and a huge backyard. It looked beautiful from the highway, though I didn't much notice that until I started getting better at drawing. But I always loved the pool and used it a lot during the summer.

Like most boys my age, I loved video games back then. That was my *thing*. School bored me, despite my parents gushing over how *wonderful* Mill Valley schools were and how I'd go on to some big university someday. Did they ever ask me what I wanted? Oh, hell, no! By the time I'd turned twelve, I knew what I wanted to do—design graphics for video games. I could draw. So could my older brother. Adults said it was genetic because our dad was an architect and all. A gift, they said. Whatever the reason, we could create almost anything with just a pencil and paper.

But, and here's the *big* but—my brother was "different." All the doctors said Austin presented "autism-like" aspects, but none would officially diagnose him as being on the spectrum. His uniqueness sent them scrambling for their medical journals to research similar cases, and they did find a few others around the world, but not many. They theorized—because doctors need labels for everything—that kids like Austin had most likely been erroneously diagnosed as autistic and treated as such, which was why there was so little authentic documentation available.

Even when I was old enough to understand that my big brother was "different," he'd never spoken a single word and hated being touched. He'd mostly accepted Mom bathing him without having a screaming fit, but if he did start screaming, it scared the hell out of me. He'd make this screeching sound, like somebody strangling a bird, and my heart would just about

2

explode with fear. Fortunately, those mega fits didn't happen often.

Whatever it was that made Austin "different," my parents had to adopt methods and skills for taking care of him. So did I, but those "skills" didn't help against jerkwads at school who called my brother a retard.

Yeah, I admit it, Austin embarrassed me. Other guys talked about how badass their big brothers were, and mine was "different." I didn't understand why he was different, but I did know those kids were dissing my family, so what was I supposed to do except punch 'em out? That's how I got a rep early on for being a "troubled kid." Since when did standing up for your brother make you troubled?

Once, when he was pulling me off a kid I'd been fighting, the principal told me I'd come to a bad end if I didn't change. "Learn to control your temper, Colton."

Did I have friends in those early grades? Yes and no. After some kids got used to Austin being around, they'd come over for birthdays and play dates. We always had a blast, especially in the pool during the summer. But as I moved up in grades, I got into more fights because of kids using the "R" word about Austin. Suddenly, even my friends' parents didn't want me at their homes, and they always seemed to have "something planned" when Mom invited their kids to hang with me. Defending my brother turned me into an angry, lonely kid. Sure, I could've laughed every time someone used the "R" word, and I even did a few times. But later, I'd feel guilty for letting the kid diss my brother and I'd punch him out anyway. I got called "Psycho Boy" by one kid I beat up in the fourth grade and that name stuck to me like gum.

I have to admit that, despite all my anger, Austin still intrigued me. He could look at something that was backwards and figure out what it was, even complex words he didn't know the meaning of. He also loved looking into mirrors - not at himself, but at the room behind him, so my parents installed mirrors all over the house because those mirrors calmed him. He even watched TV reflected in a mirror—mostly science shows, which I thought was strange. Most of the time, when we were together, he'd stare at my reflection, rather than directly at me, which I found pretty creepy. Like I said, Austin was different.

His biggest obsessions, hands down, were rain and rainbows. He *lived* for rainy days. He'd stand at the window of his upstairs room and watch the raindrops fall, his expression immobile as a rock.

At first, Mom tried to draw him away from the window and get him to play with a toy or color something. "C'mon, sweetie, you've been watching the rain for hours. Aren't you bored yet?"

She would gently nudge him, but he always shook her hand loose and continued staring at the rain as though it held all of life's secrets. When mom made the mistake of trying to force him, the choking-bird screech erupted, and my heart would start pounding. I'd run into the room to find Austin with his fists clenched, looking at mom and screaming bloody murder. The first time this happened I was only four years old, but I still remember saying to her, "He likes the rain, mommy."

I'd seen him do the staring thing before and, young as I was, I understood that this was Austin's "thing." Rain. In truth, I *thought* it was the rain until I was seven and he was ten. That's when I realized it was the *rainbow* he waited for. When that realization struck me one day, I put aside my video game console and entered his room. I'd heard the rain letting up and wondered what he would do when it stopped.

He stood by his window as usual. Then he did something I'd never seen before—he turned to me and pointed outside. I don't think Austin had ever looked straight at me before (like I said, he usually looked at my reflection in a mirror.) I walked past his bed and stood beside him. Outside, the rain had become light showers, and a rainbow had appeared in the distance. It stretched across the sky and seemed to touch down right smack in the woods blanketing Mount Tam.

And that's what Austin pointed at.

"You like rainbows, don't you, Austin?"

Of course, he didn't answer me. He lowered his arm and strode to his drawing table, shoved a pile of blocks onto the carpet and pulled out some blank paper. Then he sat on the floor, legs folded under him, and began to draw. Curious, I eased nearer to watch. With Austin you never knew if sudden movements might set him off. I slid his desk chair over and sat beside him.

What had always seemed weird to me was the direction Austin drew. He was right-handed, like me, but I either started in the center of the paper or tended to draw like I wrote, from left to right. Austin began on the right side of his paper and drew from right to left. At first, I was tempted to try and correct him, but after teachers gave up having him write his name because he always wrote it backwards, I ignored his unusual method. Like I said before, "backwards" was kind of his thing all around.

5

Within twenty minutes, he'd created an amazing likeness of the mountain forest outside his window. The rainbow looked so realistic I reached out to touch it. Austin set aside his colored pencils and sat back, staring at the image as though mesmerized. Then he looked at me. *Straight* at me. He was trying to tell me something. I didn't understand it then, not until years later, but he *was* trying to communicate.

Hell, I was only seven. What was I supposed to do? I just said, "Super cool picture, Austin."

He stared a moment longer, as though seeing right through me. Then he looked back out the window, and I followed his gaze. The rainbow had vanished. I turned back and almost gasped. For the first time in my life, Austin's face displayed a trace of emotion—sadness.

That was the first of a hundred rainbow drawings my brother crafted, each more photo realistic than the previous. He had the gift all right. He also liked to free-hand draw some of my comic book covers, especially *Reverse Flash* or *Bizarro Superman* comics (which were his favorites), and he reproduced them with stunning perfection. Both comics involved reverse versions of the superheroes.

Occasionally, when he stood at the window staring out at the woods, I'd join him, hoping I might see what he saw. Sometimes at twilight, I'd see movement among the trees, like shadows shifting places. It was probably caused by the setting sun, but I imagined monsters roaming around out there and felt a little freaked out.

But Austin would stand at the window till well after dark as though he was listening for something. I never heard a sound, and I don't think he did, either. On rainbow days, I'd see him tilting his head slightly from side to side. He'd keep his body rigid and his gaze riveted on whatever he saw out there, but I never spotted anything except the rainbow above the forest.

My parents did everything they could for him. My mom tried to bond with Austin by coloring with him. But the moment she praised him with even a slight pat on the back, he recoiled like she was a snake. I saw how much that hurt her. True, she's the only person Austin allowed to dress him and help him with bathing and other personal stuff. But he never hugged her, and even back then I saw how much she needed him to love her. Now, after everything that's happened, I know he *did* love her. He just wasn't able to show it. But I'm getting ahead of myself. I better get to that horrible day when Austin disappeared.

It was the only time my mother ever hit me.

Chapter 2

I Hate You, Austin

I was twelve by then and had been a "troubled kid" from the first grade. Middle school only made things worse. The little snot-brains in my class loved to mock me because of Austin. He'd be in a special car seat when mom picked me up from school. There was no mistaking he was my brother. We both had the same thin features and scraggly mop of untamed brown hair. I had grown curly bangs that covered my eyes so I wouldn't have to look at anything painful, but Austin liked his hair trimmed, so his eyes were visible. They were hazel like mine.

At first, Mom picked me up from middle school every day, and my life was beyond miserable. Just the sight of my fifteen-year-old brother strapped into a car seat like a freakin' toddler sent my so-called friends into gales of laughter. I burned red with embarrassment and finally told Mom I'd walk home from school. She said no at first but accepted the inevitable after I snuck out the back one day to avoid her car.

By then, I had my own cell phone, and she blew it up like crazy trying to reach me, but I switched it off as I trudged up the steep back roads to my house. I confess, I was wiped out when I got home, staggered upstairs, and crashed onto my bed. I knocked out like a light in the middle of Mom's lecture about how worried she'd been and ended up sleeping right through dinner.

After that she agreed to pick me up at the halfway point between school and home so no one would see Austin.

The day my brother disappeared was a rainy Saturday, and Casey—one of the few friends I still had—was hanging out at my house. He was in my grade, about the same size as me, with blond hair and blue eyes. He played soccer, but sports—except the video game kind—pretty much bored me.

Casey and I battled each other on my X-Box and ate junk food. My mom wouldn't let me play the really violent games, but I had a few T-rated ones and that day everything was going pretty well until midafternoon when Austin started screeching.

"The hell is that?" Casey stared at me with his mouth hanging open.

I realized that all the other times Casey had been over, Austin had stayed quiet in his room.

Not this time.

My whole body tensed up and I felt my ears burn. "Uh, my brother."

Casey's eyes bulged. "Your *big* brother?"

I nodded, anger surging through me. Once again, Austin was embarrassing me in front of a friend.

The screeching increased.

"Jeez," Casey muttered. "Sounds like somebody choking a cat."

It was a joke. I knew it was a joke. But the "troubled kid" part of me rose to the surface. "Shut your mouth!"

Casey looked at me like I was "different," too. "Dude, I know he's weird, but wow, that screaming is crazy. Your brother *is* a retard."

I dropped my game controller and Casey barely had a moment to cover his face with his hands before I landed the first punch. It glanced off his raised arms and I tackled him off the chair, completely out of control. All he could do was keep his arms up and curl into a ball while I pummeled him.

Next thing I knew, my mother was dragging me backward and yelling in my ear, "Colton, stop! You're hurting him!"

My fists struck empty air, but I kept swinging until Casey lowered his arms and gave me such a stunned look that my anger deflated.

What the hell had just happened?

Mom was pretty strong for a small woman, but then she'd had lots of experience restraining me over the years. She let go and stepped between us.

"What's going on in here?" Mom demanded, hands to her hips, mouth turned downward in an angry frown.

"He went psycho on me, Mrs. Bowman."

"Is that true, Colton?" Mom glared at me.

I could see she believed him.

Casey pulled himself together, wiped his bloody nose with a sleeve, and stood behind Mom, glowering at me. I knew he wasn't going to admit what he'd said. I could've snitched, but what for?

"Yeah, it's true," I mumbled, lowering my gaze to my bare feet. "I don't know what happened."

Mom sighed loudly, exasperated. Every time I'd been in a fight since first grade, I'd told her it was because the other kid was mocking Austin. She complained to the school the first few times, but they always told her they couldn't control what other kids said, and since Austin wasn't even a student at that school, they were under no obligation to take action. I, however, *was* a student there and apparently—according to the administration —had an obligation to keep my fists to myself, no matter what the other kids said to me.

After numerous failed attempts to get action from my school, Mom's standard response became, "Just ignore them."

Easy for you to say, Mom.

By this time, Austin had stopped screeching. It was almost as though he'd acted out on purpose just to ruin my day. Sometimes I hated him so much I couldn't even think straight. And then I'd hate *myself* for those feelings. Yeah, I was troubled, all right, but I was about to get a whole lot worse.

Mom lifted my chin with one hand so she could look me in the eye. I resented that, but I was already in enough trouble, so I tried my best to meet her gaze.

"I'm taking Casey home," she said, her voice sounding weary and angry at the same time. "I have to explain to his mother why my son can't keep his fists to himself."

I flinched but didn't pull away.

"I'll be gone no more than twenty minutes. Watch your brother. For some reason he's more agitated than usual. Can you manage that small duty?"

I nodded, and she released my chin.

Casey gave me a look like I should be locked up and then followed my silent mother from the room. I stood in front of my flat screen TV and stared through the door into the hallway. I heard the front door open and close and then Mom's car engine revving in the driveway.

I guess that's it for Casey. He'll tell everyone at school I went psycho, and everything will start all over again.

Because of Austin!

Anger boiled up within me. I stomped out into the hall and barged into Austin's room, shoving the door so hard it slammed against the wall. Austin didn't even notice. He stood at his window staring out at another freaking rainbow! The showers had lessened and there was blue in the sky above the mountain —and that stupid rainbow!

"What the hell were you screaming about?" I shouted. "I just lost another friend 'cause of you!"

He didn't turn, didn't budge. He was dressed in jeans, a cartoon tee shirt, and Reeboks. His hands were on the window glass, his gaze fixated on that rainbow arching above the tree line.

He just stood there like he wasn't ruining my life, and I couldn't take it!

I strode forward and grabbed his shoulder, spinning him around. It didn't occur to me till later that he should have screamed when I touched him, but I was too pissed off to notice. I'd never wanted to punch my brother as much as I did that day.

"I hate you, Austin. I super hate you so much. I wish you were dead! Why don't you just disappear?"

His face displayed no reaction. But he raised his left arm

12

and pointed out the window at the rainbow. Always the damned rainbows!

I probably should've looked, but it was just another rainbow, so why bother? Sure, it seemed brighter than usual, but the rain had been super heavy, and I was too wound up to care, anyway. I cursed and spun around, slamming his door as I exited. I stormed into my room and switched off the TV. Then I flopped onto my bed and stared at the ceiling, struggling to calm down.

Why had I gotten so mad? Maybe it was because things had been getting better. Kids at school hardly ever mentioned Austin anymore. He went to a special school and with Mom no longer picking me up, it was like he didn't exist.

Except he did. And there had been *way* too many times he'd embarrassed me in front of my friends. Once Casey told this story at school, the "R" word would be back, big time.

I forced my breathing to slow, allowing my heartbeat to draw down to normal.

I thought about what I'd done.

And I felt bad.

I was too old not to understand that these behaviors weren't Austin's fault. I considered what his life might be like if *I* was the "different" one, and then felt guilty as hell for what I'd said to him. How would I feel to be in his shoes? I'd probably shriek my freakin' head off every hour out of frustration.

I leaped off my bed and darted across the hall to Austin's room. His door was still closed, so I grabbed the knob. Then a strange feeling came over me.

Fear.

I flung open the door.

"Austin, I'm sor–"

I stopped dead, hand on the knob.

The room was empty. Only my reflection from the large mirror on the far wall gazed back at me.

"Austin?"

That fear wrapped itself around my heart and squeezed. I ran to his closet and yanked it open. Occasionally, Austin would use his closet to hide from the world, but he wasn't in there.

I started to tremble. I rushed out of the room into the hall, lurched forward and shoved the bathroom door open.

Empty.

Kitchen!

I sprinted along the hall and practically flew down the stairs to the ground floor.

And then my heart really did stop.

The front door hung open. Wind and leaves blew in with the dwindling showers.

I ran out onto the porch and stood in the drizzle, my gaze roaming everywhere. The driveway was empty. I heard cars racing past on Panoramic Highway but couldn't see them because trees blocked my view. In the distance, that super bright rainbow reached down from the sky to grasp the treetops along the slope of Mount Tam.

Oh, no...

I ran. My bare feet kicked up splashes of water as I pelted down the driveway and up Marin View Avenue. Light rain sluiced off my face and soaked my clothes, but I didn't even notice.

My only thought was Austin.

I arrived, panting and wheezing, at the Highway and gazed

across at the mountainside below. I had to wait for a few cars to zip past and then I crossed the street in a flash.

I ran, following the Panoramic Trail into the woods. Still no sign of my brother. I got a mean-ass stich in my side, but I didn't care. I kept running down that trail like a jackrabbit eluding a fox.

Small rocks and sticks dug into my feet, but I ignored the pain. The rainbow beckoned to me in the distance, always looming large and out of reach. I left the paved trail and dashed through the undergrowth in what I was sure was the right direction. I stopped and doubled over, gasping for breath. The diminishing rain fell in scattered droplets that bounced off the tree branches and struck me on my back and head. Sucking air in loud gulps, I stood upright and brushed dripping curls off my forehead.

"Austin!"

The damp and cold had seeped into my bones and my voice came out like a quaver.

"Austin!"

I stared ahead through the trees. The silence creeped me out and the rainbow still looked as far away as it had from the highway.

Of course, you can't find a rainbow, my frantic mind told me over and over. *But Austin doesn't know that!*

I sprinted through the trees. Branches scraped my face and arms. Even though the soles of my feet bled from sticks and scrapes, I felt no pain. Only remorse.

I searched for hours, but Austin was gone.

Chapter 3

I Didn't Hurt Him, Dad

I t was getting dark by the time I found my way home. I was spent, soaked, dirty, and bleeding from cuts and scrapes all over my body. I'd only been wearing a tank top and workout shorts when I'd run from the house and all my exposed skin was scratched to hell.

Flashing red and blue lights pulsed across my driveway and the house blazed with light as I trudged up to the front door. Of course, Mom had called the cops. What else would she have done? I gripped the knob hesitantly. How could I face my parents?

I stepped into the foyer.

Mom and Dad stood talking with a cop in a blue uniform. They fell silent when I entered and stared a moment in shock. It was like time stopped for a few seconds. Mom had clearly been crying. Dad had one arm around her waist and looked like he'd been crying, too.

What have I done?

That was all I managed to think before Mom disentangled herself from Dad and threw her arms around me. She didn't even seem to care how dirty, wet, and bloody I was.

"Oh, Colton, thank God!"

Her voice cracked with emotion, and she squeezed me like she never had before.

I didn't return the hug.

She let me go and Dad stood before me, the cop at his side.

Mom's gaze was fixed over my shoulder. "Where's Austin?"

"He's gone."

Mom's hand flew to her mouth, and Dad stiffened.

"What do you mean gone, son?" Dad was tall and rugged-looking and I'd never seen him look scared before now.

"When I...went to check on him...his room was empty," I haltingly explained. "The front door... was open and he was... gone."

Mom gasped.

"I searched everywhere for him, all through the woods, but I couldn't find him. I'm sorry, I'm *so* sorry." Tears erupted from my eyes.

There was a long moment of silence.

"You had one simple job to do." Mom raised her hand and slapped me. Hard. Right in the face. It sounded like the crack of a whip.

Sharp pain slammed into my brain. I staggered and would've gone down, but the cop bounded forward to catch me.

Dad threw his arms around Mom and held her back. "Leslie!"

I touched my stinging cheek with one hand. My parents had never hit me before. I stared at Mom in disbelief. She seemed stunned by what she'd done and tried to reach for me, but I bolted past her and took the stairs two at a time. I ran into the bathroom, slammed the door, and locked it. Then I collapsed to the cold tile floor and sobbed.

After I'd showered, I let Dad in to bandage my feet. They were pretty torn up. He didn't say much while he rolled the bandages around each foot and taped them down, but that wasn't unusual for him. He was the quiet type and usually just hung out and let me do the talking. But there was nothing to say that night. Yeah, I could have confessed that I'd driven Austin from the house, but I didn't. It was almost like by not admitting it I could convince myself it didn't happen.

After Dad put me to bed, he said, "The police want to know if there's anything else you can tell them."

I lay under my blanket shivering like a leaf—not from cold, but from fear, like I was freaking out from panic. I couldn't control the tremors.

"About what?"

Dad shuffled uncomfortably. He was still wearing his dress shirt and tie and hadn't even worried that they got wet and bloody when he'd bandaged me up. That meant he was really spooked because Dad was a neat freak to the max.

"Your, um, your mother told the officers what happened between you and Casey and, well, how..."

He trailed off.

"How psycho I acted?" I couldn't hide the bitterness in my voice.

Dad's face crumbled into embarrassment. "No, Colton, not at all. Just that you were really angry when she left you alone with Austin and..."

He stopped again, as though what he didn't say was so bad, he *couldn't* say it.

Then I knew.

Disgust filled my heart. "It's because of the fights at school, isn't it? The cops think I hurt him or..."

This time *I* couldn't finish. The cops thought I might have got so mad that I killed my brother!

"No, son, it's just, well, they have to consider every possible scenario in their investigation." Dad paused again. "They'll be back tomorrow to take your statement."

My statement. Sounded like a freaking episode of CSI or something! My heart thumped wildly, and I gripped the blanket covering me.

"I didn't hurt him, Dad. I swear it!"

"I know. You love Austin as much as we do."

What could I say to that, after what I'd done?

"I'd like to sleep now, if that's okay?"

"Of course, son. Thank you for trying to find him. The police will have men out in the woods all night, and they've sent his photo around to other police agencies."

"Why?"

Dad stopped at the door, his hand to the light switch. "In case he was kidnapped. Covering all the bases."

He flicked off the light and stepped into the hall, closing the door behind him.

Kidnapped?

Oh, Austin, I'm so sorry!

I cried myself to sleep.

Police were in and out all weekend. The Marin County Sheriff's got involved, too. Both agencies questioned me, and both thought I was lying. Kids aren't stupid like so many adults want to think. We can read people pretty well.

"Let's go through it again, son," the Mill Valley detective intoned like a robot. His name was Carter, and he looked middle-aged, tired, and hardass.

"I'm not your son," I mumbled, my temper rising. Jeez, I'd already told him everything three times!

"Colton." That was Dad. He stayed with me during the "interrogation," but hadn't said anything before now.

I glanced at him. We were in the living room. Dad sat in his favorite stuffed chair while I slouched on the sofa. The cop stood staring down at me like I was a science exhibit.

To my relief, Dad turned to the officer. "Detective Carter, my son has already told you what happened. Maybe you need to clarify what you're looking for."

I sagged with relief. At least, until the cop said, "Very well, Mr. Bowman." He looked straight at me. "Did you hurt your brother, Colton?"

"That's enough," Dad said with quiet finality.

"Mr. Bowman, Austin is missing. I must ask these questions. If Colton has nothing to hide, he simply needs to answer them."

My stomach was twisted into knots, and I really wanted to punch that cop, big time. I glanced at Dad again.

He looked uncomfortable. "Answer his questions, son."

"No, I never hurt my brother."

Except with my words.

"Did you and your brother ever fight?"

"No. He wasn't that kind of brother. We drew together. That's all he liked doing."

Carter looked long and hard at me. "You ever do anything with Austin that might be considered inappropriate?"

Inappropriate? I knew the word, sure, but I had no clue what the guy was suggesting. Dad must have because he jumped up from his chair and stepped in front of me.

"We're done here."

Carter eyed Dad as though suspecting him of wrongdoing. Then he folded up his little notebook and slipped it into his pocket. "I have to ask these questions, Mr. Bowman."

I couldn't see Dad's face because his back was to me, but I'd never heard such anger in his voice. "You're suggesting something that's beyond the pale."

I peered around Dad's back and saw the cop trying to appear sympathetic. "It does happen, Mr. Bowman, more often than you think."

"Not in my family."

"Mr. Bowman, you and your wife told me that Austin did not have a habit of wandering off."

"That's correct."

"And yet something drove him from this house yesterday," Carter went on solemnly. "I'd like to know what that was. Wouldn't you?"

Dad said nothing and I really wished I could see his face. Was he wondering about me? Did he think I might have hurt Austin?

"We're going to do everything we can to find your son, Mr. Bowman. Have a good day." Carter leaned slightly to one side so he could make eye contact with me. "Colton."

Then he left the room.

Dad stood staring into the foyer. I rose and circled around him. My hands shook.

"Dad, does he think I did something to Austin?"

Dad looked startled, as though he'd forgotten I was there. "No, son."

"What did he mean by 'inappropriate'?" I had this sick feeling in the pit of my stomach that I already knew the answer, but it was too horrible to say out loud.

"Nothing." Dad finally looked down at me and placed one hand on my shoulder. "Grab your jacket. We're going to search the woods."

I hurried upstairs as fast as my sore feet allowed.

Dad and I spent most of the day in the woods, searching alongside the police.

The rain had washed away any footprints Austin might have left in the muddy ground, and I couldn't remember which way I'd gone, where I'd searched, or even how I'd found my way home. Every tree looked the same, every clearing identical. There was no sign of him anywhere.

Mom still couldn't look me in the eye. She did come into the kitchen early in the day while I sat staring at a plate of leftover spaghetti and mumbled, "I shouldn't have hit you. I'm sorry." Then she was gone.

Those might have been the last words she said to me for months, but everything became such a blur that I couldn't remember much after a while.

By Sunday night, with nothing new on Austin, I'd drifted into a funk and refused to talk. I sat in my brother's room and stared at his myriad rainbow drawings. I didn't even eat dinner.

The search went on for two weeks, almost nonstop. Austin's photo was all over the news. Cops, sheriff's guys, and park rangers combed the woods daily. The San Francisco police department circulated his picture. Nothing turned up. Other than his room, there was no sign that Austin Bowman had ever existed.

At the end of the two weeks, I was in the kitchen snagging a soda when I heard the head detective—that Carter guy—talking to Mom and Dad in the foyer. I crept into the adjacent hallway and listened.

"Do you have to call off the search?" Mom sounded like fragile crystal that would crack at any moment.

"I'm afraid so, Mrs. Bowman. We've found no trace of him in those woods."

"What about a cougar?" Mom had expressed that concern to Dad a number of times.

"We'd have found some evidence by now." The man paused, and I listened harder in case they began whispering. "The most likely scenario, Mrs. Bowman, is that Austin was abducted after he ran from the house."

"How?" Dad asked. "Colton ran out right after him. He'd have seen someone take him."

"Colton *said* he ran out right after, but we don't have a clear timeline. You were gone twenty minutes, Mrs. Bowman. If

Austin left the house right after you did, that's plenty of time for someone to pick him up on Panoramic Highway."

"But why?"

There was a long pause.

I held my breath.

"There are a lot of sick people out there who abduct kids for all kinds of reasons, none of them good."

"What are you saying, detective?" Mom's voice was barely a whisper.

"I'm sorry, Mr. and Mrs. Bowman, but we may not find Austin alive."

The can of soda slipped from my hand and thumped onto the hardwood floor, rolling down the hall with a *clunk, clunk, clunk* sound. Dad poked his head around the corner and saw me. I stared at him, my eyes welling with tears. Mom and Carter stepped up beside him and gazed at me in silence. Dad broke away and pulled me into a tight hug.

"We won't give up, Colton. We'll never give up."

Except Mom did give up. She withdrew into herself and declined to talk to anyone. We became a family of zombies. I refused to go to school. I either sat in Austin's room and stared at his drawings or spent hours in the woods searching for some sign of him. I didn't believe my brother was dead. I couldn't believe that. I'd *never* believe that.

Was I depressed? That's what every shrink in Marin County told my parents, and I mean *every* one. I'm pretty sure I cussed out all of them. They gave me tests, or tried to, including that stupid inkblot thing you see in every TV show on earth. I said every inkblot looked like Austin. These people didn't understand that I wasn't depressed. I felt *guilty* because I'd made Austin leave, and it was my responsibility to bring him back. Somehow.

The last shrink I went to was Dr. Bernstein, an old lady with wavy gray hair and reading glasses that hung around her neck by a chain who looked a bit like my grandma in Colorado. She nailed it.

"I agree with you, Colton," she said, leaning back in a huge leather chair that practically smothered her.

I sat next to her in what I have to say was a super comfy recliner. Her office was filled with cool stuff from the movies. She was a collector, she'd told me when I first walked in and ogled everything. There were posters and props, mostly from *Star Wars* films. Turned out she was best buds with somebody out at Skywalker Ranch who gave her all the nifty stuff. But I didn't let the coolness of her place distract me, nor her resemblance to Grandma. I refused to cooperate with her tests, just like I had with all the other shrinks.

And she saw right through me.

"You're not depressed," she said, gazing at me with compassion. "You feel guilty. Would you like to talk about it?"

I don't know why. Maybe it was the Force or something, or maybe because I loved my grandma so much. Whatever the reason, I broke down and cried. Right there in front of a Darth Vader helmet staring me down from her desk.

She didn't freak out at a boy crying. She didn't tell me I was too big to cry. She just handed me a box of Kleenex and sat back in her chair. I snatched a fistful of tissue and wiped my eyes. And I told her everything. My whole life. How Austin had ruined my friendships. What I'd said to him. Everything. She took it all in until I had no more tears, or words, left.

"Do you feel better now, Colton, for having told me?"

I nodded. I really did feel better. I'd kept everything inside since the disappearance and now I felt like the steel hand squeezing my heart had finally loosened. Not let go, though. That would never happen until I found Austin. But it was like I'd been suffocating and could finally breathe again.

"You can't tell my parents."

Mom already hated me. If she knew what I'd said to Austin, she'd never speak to me again.

Dr. Bernstein nodded. "If that is your wish, Colton. What we talk about stays between us. But I do think, at some point, you should tell them everything."

I shook my head. Dad might understand, but Mom... no way.

"Your anxiety level is extremely high," she went on, her tone casual, like she was talking about us having a cup of cocoa. "If I prescribe you something, would you take it?"

I'd tried some of the anti-depressants the other doctors prescribed, if only to keep my mother from hovering every second like a helicopter. But the meds dulled my mind and made me feel weird. They made me not want to search for Austin.

That I couldn't handle.

I told this to Dr. Bernstein.

"These pills are to relax you, Colton, to help you sleep," she went on in that soft voice I liked. "You only need to take one if you feel really stressed."

I considered a moment. Mom was mad because I threw away the other pills. Maybe if I agreed to take these, she'd get off my case.

"If they make me feel like not searching for Austin, they go down the toilet." I stared long and hard at her. I needed her to know I meant business.

She smiled. The wrinkles around her mouth almost danced. It was a smile that made me think she really cared about me. The other doctors had been all business—Mr. Potato head-smiles for show only.

"Sounds like a fair deal."

She raised one wrinkled fist and stretched it out toward me like the guys do at school. I made a fist and bumped hers.

I did take the pills once in a while when I felt super stressed out, and I ended up finishing seventh grade by independent study because I'd missed so much instruction. I was also way too frazzled to face the other kids at school, especially after all the media coverage about Austin's disappearance. Much of it had been directed at me and whether or not I'd told the truth about what happened that day.

My weekly visits with Dr. Bernstein gave me an outlet to vent my feelings, because at home we didn't talk. The house was so quiet, it was like living with ghosts. I hated being there. Even my thirteenth birthday was a drag, despite Mom baking a half-assed cake and Dad giving me a laptop computer of my own. Nothing helped. I was lost without my brother, so whenever I wasn't doing schoolwork, I searched the woods.

At first, I went on my own. When I walked off the trails into the forest, I'd use string to mark the way back. But after a while, I could navigate through the trees just by looking at them. I'd never cared much about nature, so I hadn't paid any attention, but now I saw that every tree was different—just like every person was different. The markings on the bark, the colors of the needles, the thickness of the branches—every tree was unique.

I pretty much saw no one during those few months. Except Casey. Turns out he really *was* my friend. A few weeks after Austin disappeared, Casey dropped by my house. I was in Austin's room when Dad stuck his head in to ask if Casey could come up.

I really didn't want to see him because his face would be a painful reminder of that day. But then I thought of what Dr. Bernstein and I had talked about—the need to make amends. My guilt would never go away unless I could find Austin and apologize, until I knew for sure that he forgave me. She'd said, "He probably forgave you on the spot, Colton."

But hoping that Austin would forgive me, and seeing it in his eyes, were two different things. That's why I had to find him.

But *I* could forgive Casey, and maybe he needed it as much as I did.

"Send him up."

Dad nodded and left the room.

A few minutes later I heard a throat clearing. I'd already slipped away, lost within Austin's drawings, wondering where he might have gone. I looked up. Casey stood in the doorway. He wore a thick jacket, so I guessed it must be cold outside.

"Hey." He eyed me through his raggedy blond bangs and looked really embarrassed.

"Hey."

There was a long moment between us.

"I'm sorry, Colton, for, you know, what I said." His voice was low and quiet, not loud and rowdy like usual.

"It's okay. I'm sorry for pounding you."

He stepped into the room and looked around. "I never been in here before."

I didn't know what to say. I wanted to be left alone, but then, maybe some part of me wanted a friend, too. Not sure why, I held up Austin's stack of drawings. "Austin drew these."

Casey took them. His eyes widened with surprise as he rifled through them. "Wow! These are amazing. He drew as good as you."

I felt a burst of anger. "*Draws*. He's not dead, Casey!"

Casey looked mortified. "I didn't mean…"

"I'm sorry. I know you didn't."

He handed the papers back, but I didn't meet his gaze. I had the feeling he'd know it was me who drove Austin away and I wasn't ready for anyone else to know that yet.

"Your dad told me you're doing independent study."

I nodded again. I was becoming the master of non-verbal communication, but I kept my eyes on the sheaf of drawings in my trembling hand.

"Um…."

When he didn't say anything more, I looked up.

His blue eyes regarded me with uncertainty. "Can I, um… well, everybody says you're crazy to go into the woods every day, but…I don't and….well, if you…you know…want company, I'm down."

My whole body stiffened with shock, and I couldn't speak. We stared at each other a long moment. My first thought was that he was messing with me. But those blue eyes told a different story. He really *did* want to help.

"You don't have to."

"I want to."

"Thanks."

Another long pause.

"So what time are we going out?" He tilted his head toward the window.

I studied his clothes in more detail this time. He not only wore the heavy jacket, but jeans and hiking boots. He'd come over here hoping I'd let him go with me. His choice of clothes proved to me what friendship looked like. Guys can't always say it, but we figure out how to show it.

"Right now."

I went to grab my jacket.

We never found any clues about what happened to Austin. I know the police thought he might have been abducted before he reached the woods, but I didn't think so. The way he stared at the forest that day—or the rainbow, or both—convinced me that the woods had something to do with his disappearance.

But what?

The police hauled in several "shady characters," as they called them—people reported as "in the vicinity" the day Austin vanished. One was even an ex-con who'd done time for burglary and grand theft auto.

Mom, Dad, and me were called down to the station to what's called a "lineup." The three people in question had probably been interrogated up the wazoo, but no one told me any details or showed me photos. Detective Carter asked us to sit behind two-way glass and look at six men standing behind it.

"Look hard," he admonished in that quietly gruff tone that seemed to be his signature voice. "Especially you, Colton." He gave me a long look. "Did you see any of these men the day Austin disappeared?"

Mom and Dad shook their heads quickly, but I studied the face of each man carefully. I still thought it was the woods that took Austin, but what if I was wrong? If some guy had my brother, we had to find him before...no! I couldn't go there! My body tensed up and I gripped the sides of my chair so hard my fingers hurt.

I couldn't decide which of these guys was the ex-con. I guess real ex-cons don't look like they do on TV. All six men fidgeted with discomfort, but none really looked afraid. Did that mean they were all good actors, or that they had nothing to hide? I thought about the cars that had cruised past on Panoramic Highway right before I'd crossed into the woods. Had any of these guys been driving? I honestly couldn't say. I'd been so panicked I wasn't even sure I could identify the type of car. And I'd seen no one out walking either.

I released the breath I held and shook my head.

Carter looked disappointed, maybe even a trifle angry. "You're sure, Colton? Absolutely positive?"

I studied their faces again. They all pretty much looked like the male teachers at my school—ordinary.

"I never saw any of them before."

Carter sighed with obvious disappointment. It made me

realize that he genuinely hoped one of these guys would lead us to Austin. Maybe he cared, after all.

He assured my parents the police would keep all channels open, and we headed for home. Mom looked more dejected than usual because she'd had a glimmer of hope that Austin might be found. Dad stayed silent, but I knew him. He was just as upset as Mom but fought to stay strong.

More convinced than ever that the woods were the key, I spent every single day until I started eighth grade wandering amongst the pine trees and calling Austin's name till my voice grew hoarse. Casey almost always went with me. Whenever it rained that spring and a rainbow appeared, we spent more time than usual. Of course, we never found the end of the rainbow, but we searched for it anyway. I told Casey I was sure the rainbow had drawn Austin out of the house that fateful day and then, somehow, the woods had swallowed him up. Casey looked doubtful, but being the awesome friend he was, he never laughed at my weird ideas.

By summer, the rain had long since ended and Casey went back to playing soccer. Like I said before, he loved sports and had incredible soccer skills. He wanted to play on both the high school and a travel team and needed to keep up his game. But he felt guilty leaving me behind.

As we exited the woods one sunny day in June, I stuck out my hand. Surprised, he shook it.

"What's that for?"

I squinted against the warm summer sun. Our jackets had been replaced by light t-shirts. Brushing curls from in front of my eyes, I said, "For being my friend."

Casey looked embarrassed. "Course, I'm your friend." He said it like no other possibility existed.

"I know you have soccer and other stuff this summer, and when school starts, too," I said before I could chicken out. "So, I got this from now on. You don't hafta come with me anymore."

He looked ashamed. "It's just, well, I really do wanna play and...."

"I understand. This is my thing anyway. You don't gotta give up your life for him."

"You don't either, you know."

"Yeah, I do."

He gazed at me a long moment. The blue of his eyes practically glowed in the afternoon sun. "Okay."

Before we went our separate ways, he gave me an unusually shy look, like he was afraid of what I might say. "Can we still hang out?"

I raised a fist. "You know it."

He grinned, we bumped, and then he sauntered off along the highway toward his home.

As eighth grade loomed, I made a deal with my parents. I would go back to regular school and continue seeing Dr. Bernstein, but they had to let me keep searching for Austin after school and on weekends. *And* they had to stop trying to get me into sports or some other activity. I'd given up video games because they reminded me of what I'd done, and sports had never been my thing. Neither was Boy Scouts, which Dad suggested. No, I had one goal back then—finding Austin. My parents needed to accept that.

By this time, my mother seemed to recall she had a second child—me—and flat out refused to allow me to go into the woods alone anymore. "I will not lose you, too."

But Dad, always more reasonable, reminded her that I had already been in the woods so many times, I probably knew them better than I did downtown Mill Valley. Which was true. I couldn't have gotten lost in those woods if I tried. Mom reluctantly agreed. She wouldn't hug me, though. I guess she still couldn't handle that.

Chapter 4

I Think the Rain Took Them

How bad was eighth grade? At first, it was freak-show city! No joke. You'd have thought I had three heads and ten arms the way everybody stared at me. There had been so much media coverage that most of the kids suspected I'd done something horrible to Austin.

Guess I didn't blame them. How many times had I gone off on some jerk for calling Austin the "R" word? Too many to count. They knew my temper. Wasn't hard for them to imagine me killing my brother. Casey still had my back. It didn't help his cred much, but he was a popular athlete, so no one made nasty comments when I was around him.

Mill Valley isn't a huge place and the kids loved to gossip. Had I murdered my brother? Had I sold him to human traffickers? Was he eaten by a mountain lion? Was he abducted by aliens? The rumors were endless, and I forced myself to ignore them. I only got into two fights that year, mainly because I promised my parents I wouldn't. The two guys I beat up were uber-scumbags who made *really* nasty assertions, like I'd done something sexual with my brother and that's why he'd run away. It was only then that I knew for sure what Detective Carter had meant when he suggested I might have done something "inappropriate."

After returning from suspension the second time, I kept to myself and only talked to Casey during the school day. I got passing grades so my parents wouldn't be on my case but spent every day after school—and every weekend—searching those woods. Mom and Dad had long since given up trying to push me toward college. They just tried to *not* push me into complete psychosis. Was I psychotic? That's what the other shrinks had said, but not Dr. Bernstein. She always made me feel less guilty somehow, like what I'd said to my brother was something every kid says to his brother at one time or other.

"Yeah, but every kid's brother doesn't disappear right after," I'd always remind her.

To her credit, she agreed. Dr. Bernstein was stand-up, I have to say.

By the time I was fourteen and entered Tamalpais High School, it had been a year and a half since the disappearance and everyone—even Mom—presumed that Austin was dead. I wouldn't accept that. In fact, I'd expanded my search onto the internet. I didn't have much of a social media presence. I'd had a Facebook account but shut that down before entering Tam High. Too many random people wanted to friend me just because they thought I was a murderer, which, when I thought about it, was pretty disturbing. I kept Instagram to post my artwork, but that was all.

Dad had a twenty-seven-inch Mac in his office at the house. He still had private detectives searching the country for any clue that might lead us to Austin, but so far they'd found nothing. When I asked if I could use his computer to search around on the internet, Dad agreed. I told him that there might be other kids like Austin who disappeared and maybe there would be some kind of pattern. He liked that idea and sometimes we searched together, but mostly it was just me. A few months into my freshmen year, I got lucky.

According to statistics, about one-fourth of kids "diagnosed" as on the spectrum don't talk. I'd probably heard that before but tuned it out because I resented my brother too much. Since the closest "label" for Austin was "autism," I googled "autistic kids who went missing" and my world suddenly got much larger. Apparently, out of all those who'd gone missing, one third were non-verbal, and most of them were never found. Of course, some of these kids might not actually have been autistic, just mislabeled because they were like my brother.

Clicking around, I searched some of the stories about Austin to compare them to the stories of other missing kids. Most didn't have a younger brother suspected of killing them, but none of those kids who'd gone missing lived in big cities. They lived in rural areas. Areas with trees and streams and forests. Like Mill Valley.

I found one internet story about Austin's case that really did a number on me. It detailed every single fight in my troubled-kid life, from the first grade to the ninth, and painted me as a human time bomb waiting to explode. Any parents reading this story wouldn't let me within a mile of their kids.

And the comments under the story? I don't even want to go there. I was a murderer and a whole lot more. I felt sick to my stomach reading them. How could all these people who didn't even know me think I was such a monster? Just because of some story they read? Were people really that willing to believe gossip without even looking for the truth? My parents had taught me to question everything, especially news stories, because the media always had an agenda to push. I didn't know what kind of agenda would want a twelve-year-old to be a murderer and I didn't want to know.

But then I saw the following comment and my heart nearly stopped:

I don't think you hurt Austin. My brother, Kumaka, disappeared the same day as yours. I think the rain took them.

It was dated last month, posted by 'Keilani.'

With shaking hands, I typed in a reply to the comment:

Who r u? Contact me on Instagram @ColtonArtist.

I sat back from the computer to catch my breath.

I think the rain took them.

I wondered what she meant.

Chapter 5

Did He Love the Rain?

I checked my Instagram first thing in the morning before school, but Keilani hadn't messaged me. Casey's mom and mine traded off carpooling duties because Tam High was a long way on foot, and today was my mom's turn. That meant I couldn't tell Casey what I'd learned until after we got to school.

It wasn't that I didn't trust my mom. I kept quiet for her sake. She couldn't handle any ideas that suggested Austin might still be alive.

Dad explained it to me one night. "For her, it's less painful to believe Austin is dead than to think someone has him and might be hurting him, or worse. I don't even discuss him with her anymore. Only with you."

I guess I understood, even though I could never think that way.

"Have a good day, boys," Mom said as we clambered out of her BMW.

"Thanks, Mrs. Bowman," Colton offered as he stepped from the back seat.

"Thanks, Mom." I gave her my best version of a smile. Dad and I made a deal to try and look positive for her. In my case, that meant not wearing my obsession on my face twenty-four-seven.

Mom returned the smile.

"The rain?" Casey whispered as we pushed our way through the crowded hallways toward first period.

"That's what she said."

We stopped at our lockers. My mind was so preoccupied with Keilani that I grabbed the wrong book.

"Yo, Colt, first period is English."

I noticed the algebra book in my hand and shook my head. Math was after lunch. I threw it back into the locker and slid out the thick anthology we used for English, dropping it into my backpack. I took out my phone to check Instagram. Casey leaned in. Nothing. No new follower and no message.

"Clue me in soon if you hear from her, 'kay?"

I nodded, my mind racing with thoughts of this mysterious girl who might know something about what happened to Austin.

Casey clapped me on the back. "We're gonna be late."

I didn't really care, but he needed good grades to play soccer, so I trotted along beside him. I noted from the corner of my eye several groups of kids pretending not to stare. Sadly, my "Psycho Boy" rep was still alive and well.

Classes dragged on and I had to fight the urge to check my Instagram every five minutes. But the zero-tolerance policy for phones in the classroom would have gotten me a visit to the vice-principal's office and a call to my parents. So, I forced myself to leave the phone off until lunch when Casey and I could get together and check.

Finally, the lunch bell chimed. I bolted from history class and speed-walked to the cafeteria. I spotted Casey with some of his jock buddies. They scowled at me as I approached and by the time I reached him, they'd scattered.

"They afraid to catch the psycho bug or just worried I might murder 'em?" I couldn't hide the disgust I felt at being treated like I had a contagious disease or something.

"Never mind them. Did she message you?"

I shoved my anger aside, whipped out my phone, and pressed the power button as chattering kids spilled into the cafeteria to get their food.

Casey leaned in as I opened Instagram. I brushed errant curls away from my eyes and held my breath. The little notification icon showed one message. I tapped it.

Kumaka's sister started following you.

"That's her, Casey!" My heart pounded with excitement as I opened her account and found myself gazing at the face of a young boy, maybe eight or nine years old. He looked Hawaiian.

"Look, Colt, she sent you a private message."

He pointed to the lit-up message icon in the upper right corner. I tapped it and we saw:

This is my brother, @coltonartist. He disappeared the same day as yours. We need to talk. Do you use Discord?

I thought my heart would burst from my chest. Finally, a real lead! Casey's eyes were big and round with excitement.

"Can I come over after practice and find out what she tells you?"

I nodded. The wheels in my head were turning. I didn't have a Discord account because Mom didn't trust those apps. Should I create one without telling my parents?

Casey must've read my thoughts because he said, "Uh, Colt, your dad is pretty slick on the computer. You're not thinking of trying to hide what you're doing?"

I saw the earnest look on his face. I'd spent so much time alone in my search for Austin that I somehow thought of my parents as being against me. But they wanted him back as much as I did.

"No. I'm gonna bring Dad in on this. He's already got private detectives on the hunt. Maybe they could check on this Kumaka kid too."

Casey grinned. "That's a plan. Now let's get some food. I'm starving."

I stared a moment longer at the phone screen, and then downloaded the Discord app. I was pretty sure Dad wouldn't mind as long as I told him what it was for. I created a quick profile for myself and typed my contact name into a private message to Keilani.

I'm in Cali how bout 7 my time

I waited a few seconds while Casey dragged me to the lunch line. When she didn't respond, I closed the app and slipped the phone back into my pocket.

Dad was super understanding when I told him about Keilani and Discord and her upcoming call. His detectives had turned up nothing, so he was excited to hear my news. He wasn't even worried about me using Discord. "Maybe this girl knows something that will help us."

I hoped that would be the case as we fired up Discord on the Mac and awaited the call. Casey sat anxiously beside the computer as Dad and I stared at the Discord screen like it was the answer to all our questions.

I kept checking the time on my phone, even though it was right there at the top of the computer screen. I was nervous, my mind whirling with the idea that finally, after two years, I might learn something new.

Casey and Dad talked sports, but I didn't listen. I watched as the minutes ticked by so freaking slowly that I wanted to scream. In truth, we only waited for five minutes before an incoming call popped up. It just *seemed* like forever.

I clicked on the video icon and a pretty Hawaiian girl appeared on screen. She had long black hair and a serious expression on her face.

"Colton?"

She glanced from me to Casey.

"I'm Colton. This is my best bud, Casey, and this is my dad."

I eyed Casey a moment and noted him staring at her with his mouth hanging slightly open. Casey had more interest in the girls at school than I did. Me, I couldn't care less.

"I'm Keilani," the girl said. She had a soft voice that didn't quite fit the stern look she wore, but I figured she was anxious—

she wanted to know what I knew and I wanted to know what she knew, so we were both on edge.

"Why did you say the rain took them?"

I felt Dad's hand on my shoulder. "Whoa, slow down, Colton. Let's give her a chance. Thank you for calling, Keilani. I'm Tom Bowman."

She offered a tight smile. "I'm glad Colton messaged me. I've only had my mom to talk with about Kumaka. My friends don't want to hear about him anymore."

I tried not to scowl. "Wish that was true for me. Out here the kids wanna believe I killed Austin, or something just as bad."

Dad's hand squeezed my shoulder. "Tell us about your brother, Keilani."

She explained how Kumaka, who had been nine when he disappeared, was nonverbal his whole life, like Austin. Also, like Austin, he was diagnosed as having "autism-like" aspects but was not considered part of the standard spectrum. In other words, he was "different" in a way that couldn't be quantified.

I blurted, "Did he like mirrors and other backwards stuff?"

She looked stunned. "Yes, he did. We had to put mirrors all over the house."

"What about rain?" I couldn't contain my rising excitement.

"Stared at it for hours."

"Dad, it's just like Austin." I turned to see Dad looking perked up and more alive than he had in two years.

"Go on, Keilani."

"Kumaka had a habit of wandering off," she went on as though she'd told this same story a hundred times, "so we'd never panic when he did. That day, I was in my room reading and Mom was in the kitchen. Kumaka was in his room. Or so we thought. When I went to check, he was gone."

"Was the front door open?" I asked breathlessly.

She looked surprised. "Yes. Mom and I searched everywhere. Maui is green with lots of mountains, and we live right next to one. We called the police and they searched with us, but never found a thing."

I scooted closer to the screen for no real reason except that I was eager. "Why did you say that about the rain?"

Now her face took on a thoughtful look. "Because I've been searching the internet for other kids who vanished. That's how I found Austin. There have been other missing kids and—"

"They all disappeared in the rain?"

She nodded. "Yeah."

I explained how I'd done the same search and found that it was mostly kids from rural areas who went missing.

"It's funny I didn't notice the rural thing before," she said, her voice sounding reproachful, as though she should have figured out everything by now. "You're right. No city kids have vanished in the same way our brothers did."

"Did you find out any other common factors, Keilani?" Dad asked as he leaned in over my shoulder.

"The kids who were never found were all nonverbal from birth."

I glanced at Dad. "Remember, Dad, I told you that before. That's gotta mean something."

"Do you think aliens took 'em, Keilani?" Casey asked excitedly, before Dad could reply. "Colt and me talk about that a lot."

She tilted her head as though thinking. "I've thought about

it, too, but I don't know. I just know that rain has something to do with it. Some old legends talk of kids being spirited away under cover of rain."

"By who?" I shivered at the thought.

She shrugged. "Mythical creatures like shape shifters and stuff. I don't buy that. But there has to be a rain connection that makes sense."

I paused. "I do think the alien idea might be legit." I waited for her to laugh, but she didn't. "Like...." I thought for a moment, an idea forming in my head. "Like maybe the aliens use rain to hide from our technology, radar and stuff. And they don't snatch kids from big cities because then they couldn't hide their ships so well."

She looked like she didn't think my idea had any value. "Um, maybe. Why don't you explore that angle and I'll keep searching for other missing kids. Maybe I can find a pattern we can use."

"I have private detectives searching for clues in Austin's case, Keilani," Dad said. "If you send me Kumaka's picture, I'll have them look for him, too."

Her face lit up. "Wow, that would be awesome. My mom can't afford to do that."

"I'm happy to help," Dad went on and rattled off his email address. "Just send his photo and stats and I'll get right on it."

"I will." She'd seemed deflated when the call began, but now she looked fired up. "Keep in touch, Colton. Just remember my time is three hours earlier than yours, so don't call while I'm in school."

She sounded so serious, I just nodded. Would I care if she

called me during school? No. But then, I didn't care about school.

"Later, Keilani," I said and reached for the mouse.

"Nice meeting you," Casey practically shouted, and then she was gone with a slight wave at the camera.

I turned to Dad. "That's super cool of you, Dad, helping find her brother."

Dad looked thoughtful. "I have a feeling there *is* a connection, like she said. If we find Kumaka—"

"We might find Austin," I blurted, cutting him off.

"It's something." He patted me on the back and left the office to help Mom in the kitchen.

I stared a long moment at the computer screen, thinking over everything I'd just heard.

"She's really hot," Casey murmured beside me.

I grunted. "I guess."

"Are you kidding? She's a total babe."

I turned my head to glare at him. "So? We're trying to find my brother, remember?"

Casey looked abashed and I felt bad for my sharp tone.

"Sorry, Colt. You're right. So, what's next?"

"Alien abduction."

"Huh?"

"I need to learn everything I can about it. Wanna help?"

"Hell, yeah. I can use my computer at home while you search here. We can send each other what we find."

"Sounds like a plan," I agreed, and we bumped fists on it.

47

From that moment on, I obsessed over every alien abduction story I could find. Casey had more going on in his life and didn't have as much time, but he searched too. We both kept in contact with Keilani. As promised, Dad gave Kumaka's picture and stats to his private detectives, but nothing turned up on either boy. The more I read about people who were abducted by aliens, the more I believed that was what happened to Austin and Kumaka.

"You said before that Kumaka would wander off sometimes and you couldn't find him for hours, right?" I asked Keilani one night while we were chatting.

She tilted her head in this way I'd grown to like. "Yeah, why? Did Austin do that, too?"

"No. My mom was super paranoid about Austin wandering, so she never let him out of her sight." I paused. "Except at night, when everyone was asleep."

"What are you getting at, Colton?"

I thought back on all the links I'd bookmarked over the past month. Some things that were similar in most abduction stories didn't seem to fit Austin. Or did they?

"Colton?"

I realized she was waiting for my answer. "Um, here's the thing. The people who say they were abducted, including kids, all say it happened more than once. They have, like, gaps in their memories, usually a few hours. Sometimes days."

She looked confused. "So?"

I shifted position in Dad's desk chair and leaned in closer. "So, what's the longest time Kumaka was gone?"

She considered a moment, pushing her long black hair over

her shoulder as she sat back to think. "Well, all day, but that was just once, as far as I can remember."

I nodded but said nothing. My research whirled around in my head. I saw drawings that kids had made of saucers and weird looking creatures. I saw the metal implants people said they'd found in their bodies.

"Austin was never left alone except at night, like I said," I finally spoke, articulating my thinking as I processed the thoughts. "And Kumaka disappeared at least once for up to a day."

She looked exasperated with my hesitation. "Yeah?"

It scared me to say what I was thinking, so I let out a long breath to prepare. "So, both of them could have been abducted during the hours we weren't with them and then returned before we knew what happened."

She gasped. "That's crazy, Colton."

"Why is it crazy?"

"I talked with my mom, and she doesn't believe in aliens. I don't think I do, either."

"I never much did, either, until now." I paused. "Did Kumaka draw any weird pictures? Lots of abducted kids do."

She shook her head.

Suddenly, in the face of her doubts, I began to distrust my ideas. "Can I at least send you some of the stuff I found out and you see if any of it fits?"

She still looked skeptical. "Okay."

"Thanks."

I paused again and studied her face, hoping I could count on her to follow through. Casey was right, I realized—she *was* pretty. He liked her a lot, but I didn't care about that. I only wanted to find my brother.

"Um, did you find out anything new about the other missing kids?" I asked to keep the conversation going.

She sighed, looking worn out. "I found more nonverbal kids who vanished during a rainstorm who lived in rural areas, like you said. None are really young, though, like toddlers or anything. I think the youngest I found was six. That could be important, but I don't know."

I gasped and sat up straight in the chair.

"What?"

I felt seriously out of breath, but when I could talk, I said, "Um, in my research, uh, supposedly aliens kind of play with little kids in their rooms to... I don't know, get them to feel safe or something. But the youngest age for an abductee is...six."

Suddenly, she didn't look so skeptical of my ideas. "How many of those kids are nonverbal?"

That's where my research had hit a snag. "None that I know of," I admitted. "They could talk about what they remembered."

The skepticism was back on her face.

Before she could shoot me down, I added, "But that doesn't mean they haven't taken kids like Austin and Kumaka. It's not like my brother or yours could tell us what happened."

Her face softened a bit. "I guess."

"I'm going to keep looking for clues, even if you don't believe me," I asserted before she could say anything else.

Now she looked apologetic. "I'm sorry, Colton. I don't mean to sound like that. It's just, well, aliens are pretty far-fetched."

"Maybe. But so is the idea that the rain took them."

She looked slightly embarrassed. "That's true."

"But there could be a connection. If aliens use rain to hide from our radar and stuff, that helps explain why there was rain every time. I'm still exploring that angle."

She smiled, and I gotta say it was a great smile. "Austin is lucky to have you."

I bowed my head and said nothing. If he didn't have me for a brother, he'd still be home in his room instead of who knew where. That blanket of guilt settled over me like dead weight and I told Keilani I had to go.

She looked disappointed. "Oh, okay. Call again whenever."

"I will."

I ended the call and opened my alien abduction folder. A link caught my eye, one I hadn't yet had time to explore, and I clicked on it. It was a search engine for finding alien abductees by zip code. That seemed weird to me, but hell, why not? I typed in my zip code and set the search radius for fifty miles.

One name popped up: Alysse Randall in Lucas Valley.

No age, address, or phone number. But Lucas Valley was only about thirty miles away. I pulled up the White Pages for Marin County and scrolled to the "R's."

Bingo. There was a phone number.

I went to get Dad.

Chapter 6

You're Saying My Son Is Probably Dead?

D ad was all for meeting Alysse Randall, but we had to discuss it with Mom first. That worried me, given how she shut down every time Austin's name came up, but Dad promised he'd do most of the talking.

Mom had changed a lot in the years since Austin vanished. She wasn't angry anymore, but it was like all the life had gone out of her. I sort of understood, because all the life had gone out of me, too.

She'd cut her hair short, so it almost looked like those twenties flapper girls we learned about in history class. When I'd asked her why, she just said, "Less work to take care of." She never wore makeup anymore and the worry lines on her face had intensified a bit more each day since the disappearance. She showed little interest in socializing, except with Mrs. Scatena—who lived next door—and Casey's parents.

And then there were the "looks" she gave me when she thought I wasn't paying attention. They weren't angry, like I said, but more worried or afraid. She had that "look" on her face every time I left for school or went into the woods or left to kick it at Casey's house. I finally asked Dad if he knew what it meant.

"She's scared, Colton."

"Why?"

I was almost as tall as him now and he looked me right in the eye. "Every time you leave the house, she's afraid you might never come home."

That floored me. But then, I'm not a parent. It made sense, though, when I thought it over. After that, every time I left the house, I always gave Mom a hug. The smile in her eyes told me she appreciated the gesture, even if she never expressed it in words. And she never quite hugged me back. I guess she still blamed me, deep down, for not keeping Austin safe that terrible day.

We sat her down in the family room, and I let Dad do the talking. I was stunned at how calmly Mom took the news that I —well, technically *we* because Dad was pretty much in agreement—had come to the conclusion that Austin had likely been abducted by aliens.

Dad gave her the basics, then she turned to me and said, "Tell me everything you found out, Colton."

It took about twenty minutes to go through it all, including my theory about aliens using rain to hide their ships, although I'd never found any information to confirm the idea.

"One kid said he was playing outside with his brothers and sisters when a big black space opened in the air, like a tent, and he walked through." That story had given me the shivers because I kept picturing Austin going through that same opening. "He said some humanoids talked to him for a while and then the space opened again and he walked back out. His brothers and sisters were all asleep on the field where they'd been playing. When he woke them up, they didn't remember what happened."

There was other non-alien stuff I'd picked up on some really "fringy" websites, but I didn't think any of it applied to Austin's case, so I left that info out.

Mom asked a few questions, but mostly she listened. Her deeply-lined face barely changed, so I had no idea what she was thinking. I glanced at Dad a few times, but I guessed he didn't know, either.

Finally, I told her about Alysse in Lucas Valley, how Dad had already called her, and that she'd agreed to meet with us. Of course, Alysse knew about Austin. Everyone in Marin County knew that story. She also thought my idea about abduction was a likely possibility.

Mom listened until Dad and me had nothing else to say. She sat in a large armchair with her hands on her lap and stared at us both a long moment. Then she said, "Of course, I'll go with you."

My mouth hung open and Dad didn't say a word. I almost gagged on what Mom said next.

"I'd rather have him taken by aliens over humans any day. I know what evil things humans do to children. At least, I can hope aliens haven't hurt him. So, when do we visit Alysse?"

Dad and I looked at each other in shock. We'd been so careful not to even whisper about the whole "alien thing" for fear of upsetting Mom and here she was acting pretty badass about the whole idea. Life is crazy.

Alysse and her daughter lived off Lucas Valley Road in a small, unpainted wooden house in the middle of the woods. It took almost an hour to get there over mostly one-lane roads. Towering trees surrounded their property and stone steps led up to the house. It had two stories, with pretty planter boxes outside the two upstairs windows, but compared to my place, it was like a cottage. The cool January breeze felt good against my face as I climbed the steps to the front door. After Dad rang the bell, a chime echoed through the house. I shifted from foot to foot.

When the door swung open a few seconds later, a woman and a teen girl stood framed in the doorway, both dressed in casual pants and tee shirts. The woman—Alysse—had short brown hair and wore no makeup, which made her youthful face look fresh and alive.

From Dad's phone calls with Alysse, I already knew she had a daughter my age. Emily was shorter than me, with shoulder length brown hair, big suspicious brown eyes, and lips curled into what looked like a snarl. She obviously didn't trust us.

Dad handled the introductions and Alysse ushered us inside. We'd passed a lot of luxurious homes on the way, but the Randall home had nothing fancy inside—no crystal wineglasses in display cases like Mom had at our house, no upscale original art on the walls. It was simple, clean, and cozy. I felt comfortable from the moment I walked in.

Alysse offered us fresh lemonade and we went out to talk in the backyard. Emily kept giving me the eye. Not *that* eye. The *evil* eye. I wondered if I looked like somebody who'd messed with her before.

The backyard was surrounded by tall trees that merged into woods extending outward in all directions, making the yard seem endless. I felt at home, as I always did around trees. They reminded me of Austin.

After everyone was seated with a glass of lemonade, I noticed Alysse and Emily staring at all of us in a weird sort of way.

Dad asked, "Are you all right, Alysse?"

She nodded but stared a moment longer at us. When she turned to look at Emily, the girl shook her head.

Alysse broke into an apologetic smile. "I'm sorry. We were just studying you."

All at once, I understood. "You can tell when people have been abducted, can't you?" I'd read about abductees who could do that.

Emily looked surprised, but Alysse's flat expression didn't change. "Yes. There's a change in the human aura, something that lingers after alien contact. None of you have it."

"Of course not," Mom said, a bit testily. "We're here about Austin."

"It's just that abductions tend to run in families," Alysse explained. "Both Emily and I have been taken several times."

"That's usually how it works," Emily said in a snarky tone.

"With all due respect, Alysse," Dad said with an awkward clearing of his throat, "did they leave any evidence behind to indicate you'd actually been taken?"

Alysse nodded at Emily, who rose to approach us. I pressed back into my chair. She had such an abrasive attitude, I figured she might throw a punch. She stopped in front of my dad, rolled up her left sleeve, and pointed to a divot about the size of a Skittle.

"The aliens take skin samples from us and leave these marks behind," Emily said flatly, glancing my way, as though expecting me to argue.

I didn't. I'd already read about this in my research. I leaned in to examine the small indentation. It looked just like the ones I'd seen in pictures on the internet, like someone had scooped out a perfectly neat chunk of skin.

"Do you still have your implants?" I asked.

Emily's eyes widened, like she thought I was too stupid to know about the implants.

"I read about you before we came over." I hoped she wasn't offended that I'd asked.

"You've been doing your homework," Alysse replied with a nod of approval, rising from her wicker chair and stepping closer.

Both she and Emily turned and pushed up their hair behind their right ears. Along with my mom and dad, I leaned in to get a closer look. They each had a tiny scar in the skin, no more than a sixteenth of an inch long.

They let their hair drop back into place as they turned around to face us.

Mom looked confused. "What is that mark?"

Alysse looked at me. "Tell them."

I turned to my parents. "Many abductees find a tiny piece of metal implanted somewhere on their bodies." Mom's eyes widened in shock. I hadn't told her about the implants before. "There's usually a weird membrane around the implant and the combination of metals is not like anything we make here on earth." Mom looked ready to protest, and I quickly added, "That we know of. Some people think the government is behind the abductions, so they can perform experiments and not get caught."

Mom shivered. "I think I'd prefer aliens over that."

"Me, too," Dad echoed.

"Are they still in there?" I asked Alysse.

She shook her head. "We had them surgically removed."

"Can we see them?" That was Dad.

Mom reached for his hand and held on tight.

"As Colton probably knows from his research, Emily and I received far more attention than we wanted after reporting our abductions," Alysse went on soberly.

I nodded. There were tons of stories and lots of pictures of them hiding their faces from news cameras.

"Agents showed up frequently from various government departments—including Homeland Security," Alysse continued. "They took the implants for analysis. All I have left are photos and the surgical report of their removal."

She slipped a phone from her pants pocket and swiped it open. After punching a few buttons, she held it out to us.

The image on screen showed an open palm with two tiny pieces of what looked like metal. Dad leaned in, but Mom held back. I studied that image, and several more she scrolled through. The pictures looked just like the objects I'd seen on the Net.

I sat back while Dad gazed long and hard at the photos. "I don't suppose Homeland Security ever told you what these things are?"

"Every time we contact them, they give us the runaround."

Emily expelled an exasperated breath. "Pigs."

Mom cleared her throat, and everyone turned to her. "With all due respect, how is any of this going to help us find my son?"

Dad squeezed her hand, and we waited to see what Alysse would say.

She glanced at Emily and they both sat down again.

"It might not," Alysse finally said after a long silence. "Austin has been gone for two years now, correct?"

I nodded, and saw Mom do the same.

"Travis Walton, abducted when he was twenty-two in 1975, was missing for five days before he returned. His is the longest abduction-return on record. If others were abducted for longer, they never came back that we know of."

Mom stiffened in her chair and gripped Dad's hand. "You're saying my son is probably dead?"

Alysse looked mortified. "Oh, no, not at all. It's possible your son is someone they want to study more fully, maybe for his psychic abilities."

"Uh, Austin doesn't have any psychic abilities," I said.

"That you know of," Emily put in with a smirk.

"That's enough with the attitude, Em," Alysse reprimanded her.

Emily looked pouty but didn't respond.

Alysse turned back to us. "Both Emily and I were first contacted by—" she paused as though for the right word. "For want of a better description, a ball of light in our bedrooms. The light communicated straight into my brain, and I understood that it wanted me to respond telepathically. I think that's how the aliens test the psychic abilities of humans before taking them. Austin might have scored very high."

"You think Austin was visited at night in his room?" I asked excitedly. Alysse's story confirmed what I'd told Keilani.

Alysse shrugged. "You said yourself that Austin was in his room alone every night. It's possible."

Dad shifted with discomfort. "You're saying they might have tested him first and then came back later to take him?"

"It happened to us. Maybe it was aliens that called him out into the woods that day. There are theories that some aliens can travel between dimensions. This could explain why there's been no trace of Austin."

"Between dimensions, Alysse?" Dad wore a very skeptical look on his face.

"Have you heard of the Large Hadron Collider in CERN? Scientists theorize that experiments with the Collider may soon confirm the existence of multiple dimensions."

There was a long pause while we all digested this possibility. I'd considered the inter-dimensional thing too, because of Austin having been gone for so long, but everything I'd read was pure speculation.

"What exactly did these aliens do to you?" Mom asked. I heard the tremor in her voice. She was scared. Dad pulled her closer.

"Are you sure you want to know?"

Mom hesitated, and then nodded.

"And it's okay to talk about it in front of Colton?"

"I'm almost fifteen," I snorted indignantly. "Besides, I already read about this stuff."

"Go on," Mom whispered.

Between them, Alysse and Emily described alien creatures with large eyes stripping them naked and running thin, cold fingers over their skin to test the nervous system. They'd felt their minds probed through their eyes, and other neurological tests were performed with unfamiliar equipment. Both reported having eggs extracted.

"Male abductees have sperm taken," Emily added, eyeing me with amusement and causing me to blush.

"Why do they want those things?" Mom asked, that tremble still in her voice.

Mother and daughter exchanged an uncomfortable glance.

"Some experts believe it's for the purpose of creating alien-human hybrids," Alysse replied quietly.

Mom stood up. "I've heard enough. I thought you might give me hope. But if aliens did take Austin, he's no better off than if people did." She turned to Dad. "Take me home, please, Tom."

Dad stood, and I followed reluctantly.

Looking troubled, Alysse stepped over to Mom. "I'm sorry I upset you, Leslie. The only hope I can give you is that if Austin was abducted, he might still return."

Mom offered a stiff nod and pulled Dad along toward the door leading into the house.

Alysse paused by my side and said in a low voice, "Be watchful, Colton."

I froze. "Why?"

She looked grave. "They might take you next."

A flood of fear swept through me.

She offered an encouraging smile. "Just keep your eyes and ears open."

"Okay."

She patted my arm and entered the house.

Emily sauntered up. "You on Discord?"

I nodded, still filled with dread over her mother's words.

"Wanna keep in touch? I don't have many friends."

I was stunned by her request, given her weird behavior toward me before. "Sure. I don't have many friends either."

That was how Emily became my newest Discord friend.

Where did all this research and speculation leave us? Back at ground zero: we had plenty to think about, but we didn't *know* any more about what happened to Austin than we did on the day he disappeared. Everything was guesswork and all sorts of possibilities were on the table. He could have been taken by humans *or* aliens. The rain may or may not have been important. There might be a connection between Austin and the other nonverbal kids who vanished, but since no trace of him had turned up via the police or FBI, that idea went nowhere. In my mind, so long as nothing proved him dead, he was alive, and I would find him.

After a couple more years went by, I ended up alone in that obsession. Dad stopped paying private detectives and Mom went back to not mentioning Austin's name. She kept his room exactly as it was, which I suppose was her one lifeline to hope.

And I wasn't abducted. I confess, for many months after meeting Alysse and Emily, I slept with the lights on. I'd acted all hardass at their place, but the thought of actually being the subject of those experiments scared the crap out of me.

Dad didn't believe everything Alysse had told us, but he still considered the abduction scenario a "possibility." Sure, kids vanished all the time and their bodies weren't discovered for decades. But the idea that Austin was still alive and aboard some alien ship somewhere was better than picturing him moldering away in an unmarked grave, so Dad clung to that feeble tendril of hope.

Casey got more into school stuff in addition to soccer. He moved in and out of the popular circles with ease, but those people wanted nothing to do with me. He tried to include me, but when I heard things like, "You can keep your queer boyfriend, we're outta here," I knew I had to step away, for Casey's sake.

That was the latest rumor about me, by the way. I already mentioned about the guys I punched out who said nasty things about me doing something sexual with my brother. Now, because I kept to myself and only hung around with Casey, in the eyes of my peers, that meant I *had* to be gay.

I even considered the possibility. A few girls showed some interest in me during junior year. At least, I think they were interested and not just messing with me. I was sixteen and I guess lots of the guys my age had girlfriends. But I didn't care about things like that. I had two girls who were friends—Keilani and Emily—and I wasn't interested in dating either one of them. I wasn't attracted to any girl, so I wondered if I might be gay. But I wasn't attracted to any guys, either.

I discussed it with Dr. Bernstein. "Do you think I might be gay?" I didn't know why, but I really wanted her answer. I think I trusted her more than any other adult.

"What I think is of no consequence, Colton," she answered

with a warm smile on her craggy face. "And it really isn't important, is it?"

I considered that a moment. "No, it isn't."

I simply wasn't interested in any close relationships except those I already had, and I told her that. I just wanted to be left alone. I wanted to find my brother. In my mind, everything else would fall into place after that.

I told Casey we could hang out when he had time, but not to sweat it with his other friends. We had regular Discord sessions with Keilani and Emily. Emily described her abduction episodes in greater detail, and they creeped me out because I thought about Austin. And I confess, I kept worrying if I might yet be taken. Keilani, too, became more unnerved than relieved, so we decided to stick with everyday topics and only mention the missing boys if something new turned up.

Nothing ever did.

Emily wasn't straightforward like Keilani. She was snarky as hell—not unusual for a teenager—and she had a weird habit of not calling any of us by our names. She called herself "Fringe Girl," Keilani was "Hawaiian Girl," Casey was "Cute Boy" because "you have killer eyes," and for me she'd adopted my school nickname, "Psycho Boy." Now, don't get me wrong, I was more than used to "Psycho Boy" by now and I wasn't looking for a girlfriend. However, somewhere deep down, it bothered me, just a little, that Casey got to be "Cute Boy" while I was thrown under the "psycho" bus.

I mean, I wasn't bad looking, at least compared to many of the guys at school. I didn't play sports, so I wasn't ripped like Casey, but I had a few weights at home, and I was in decent shape, despite being on the thin side. In any case, there wasn't much I could do about the nickname. After Emily pursed her lips in a snarky, but cute, way and called me Psycho Boy a few times, I got used to it.

The name became almost a term of endearment, and that ultimately took away its power over me at school. When other kids called me Psycho Boy, I just smiled and said, "You got that right." Oddly enough, my peers dropped the nickname after that. Much later, I considered the possibility that Emily had done it on purpose. She never said so, but she was pretty slick, so I'd bet money on it.

Emily and I hung out a few times during the summer months over those next couple of years. She'd even hiked the woods of Mount Tam with me to see if she could pick up an "alien vibe," as she called it. But they were just woods. Casey was too busy all the time to join us, but he hung out with us once in a while. The first time he saw Emily in person, he sized her up with a funny look on his face.

"What, Cute Boy? In the flesh, I'm too gorgeous for words?"

"No. You just look taller on Discord."

She'd glowered and he laughed, punching her lightly on the shoulder. "Gotcha, Fringe Girl."

I laughed, too. It was funny seeing Emily get a taste of her own snarky wit.

She'd finally grinned and said, "Very funny."

Keilani loved being on both the surf and tennis teams at her school. She had dark skin and a killer tan. Emily, by contrast, was pale to the point of looking like a ghost. She once joked to Keilani, "You and me should hang out for Halloween. We could be both sides of the Force."

As a group, despite how different we were, being connected

by the two missing boys made us click as a team, like we'd known each other forever. Our group Discord sessions were almost my whole social life, not counting hanging out with Casey or Emily.

My only other solace was art. My work consistently won awards and art was easily my best school subject. Straight A's across the board in that class. Everything else was B's or C's. I had to force myself—and it wasn't easy, at first—to *not* put a rainbow into every piece of art I created. But gradually, over those first three and a half years of high school, I managed to put Austin into a compartment within my brain so that he and his disappearance—and my guilt—didn't find their way into every aspect of my life.

By senior year, I'd sent my portfolio to all the schools my counselor recommended—like Cal Arts and the Art Center of Pasadena—but I only did it to please my parents. I was in the running for scholarships from a few schools, but it didn't matter. I wouldn't go. Not if it meant leaving the woods where I felt closest to Austin.

Even Keilani moved on with her life. She no longer obsessed over finding Kumaka. She was one of her school's best surfers and she had a boyfriend now. At least, she'd put "in a relation-ship" as her Facebook status. That update, coming in the fall of our senior year, hit Casey hard, especially since Keilani refused to discuss the subject. Emily had grilled her with questions about the guy, but she smiled coyly and wouldn't answer.

"All the girls think you're hot, Casey," I assured him. "Even I notice how much they stare at you."

He shrugged. "I guess. But I really like Keilani, you know? It's, like, I feel I might even love her. Crazy, huh?"

"Why is it crazy?"

"Cause we never even met in person. I mean, yeah, we talk every day, sure, and she's, like, the most amazing girl I ever met. She's funny and athletic and beautiful and she laughs at my lame jokes."

I smiled. "I know. You tell me these things every day. Sometimes twice a day."

He ignored my attempt at humor. "Do you think it's possible to fall in love with someone you only know from Discord?"

I considered his question. "I think it's about hope. You hope she might feel the same way about you and that you'd know for sure if you met her in person. It's like me with Austin. I know he's out there and I can't give up hoping I'll see him again, no matter what anybody says."

He looked at me, his eyes filled with uncertainty. "You still think he's out there?"

"Yeah, I do." I gave him a long look. "And I still think you have a shot with Keilani. The boyfriend is just a temporary placeholder."

He grinned and punched me on the shoulder. I grinned right back.

That was January of my senior year, and I was seventeen. My life continued in a holding pattern; kind of like airplanes hung up by the fog at San Francisco Airport.

Until one day everything changed, because Austin came home.

Chapter 7

This Is Only the Beginning, Colton

School was tedious that day—when was it ever anything else? What made it different was my anxiety level. It had been raining like mad the past two days, almost with the same intensity as the day Austin disappeared. Rain always increased my stress level because I'd flash back to that horrible afternoon. But today was different. As the afternoon wore on, my apprehension soared. My focus level diminished to zero. I stared out windows all day without knowing what I was looking for.

Finally, the last bell rang, and I was free. I strode through the hallway toward the exit, head down and mind fixated on the image of hard, driving rain, when I was struck by a feeling that something had changed. It jolted through me, and I froze. Though I sensed other kids staring, I didn't really see them. I looked straight ahead at the door leading out to the student parking lot. And then I bolted from the building.

Navigating Miller Avenue in my parents' BMW, I felt my

frustration rise at the slow-moving traffic. Sure, it was raining, and the road was slippery, but I tuned out that reality and fumed with anger at the cars blocking my way.

I had to get home.

Now!

I swung a hard left onto Montford Avenue. My tires slid on the slick pavement and my heart flew into my throat as the car swerved toward the oncoming traffic lane. I spun the wheel to straighten it out and then raced up Mount Tam, my breathing ragged from that close call. Once I got to Panoramic Highway, with only one lane in either direction, the going became slower still. I had to fight the urge to honk the horn and force cars out of my way.

Hurry up, people!

I gripped the steering wheel with such intensity my knuckles turned white. The rain had turned to light showers and when I turned a corner, the sight of an enormous rainbow greeted me. Just like on the day Austin disappeared, it stretched across the sky and down into the sloping woods. I almost went off the road staring at it and had to jerk the wheel hard to the right to avoid an oncoming SUV. The driver laid on his horn as he passed, but I didn't care.

Our driveway was empty, which meant Mom was out. I slammed on the brakes and screeched to a stop, then killed the engine. Leaping from the car, I sprinted for the front door. I needed to get to Austin's room.

I threw open the door and took the stairs two at a time, shaking water like a dog from my huge mop of hair. I didn't hesitate. I grabbed the knob and pushed open his door.

The room was empty.

I sagged with disappointment. What had I expected? That by some magic, Austin would be up there playing with his toys or sketching the rainbow, as though the past five years hadn't happened?

And yet the feeling that had called me home persisted. *Something* had changed. I turned my head and gazed out the window at the stunningly vivid rainbow in the distance. Every glittering strand shimmered with vibrant life. It was a perfect copy of the super bright rainbow Austin had been staring at the day he vanished.

Like iron to a magnet, I shuffled forward to stand before the glass. Water dribbled past my field of vision, but that rainbow held my gaze.

Then I had the urge to look down.

My heart stopped.

For real.

Austin stood in the driveway looking up at me as though he'd never been gone.

I stiffened for a split second, afraid I was hallucinating. How Austin looked didn't even register; all I saw in that moment was my brother gazing up at me. I dashed out of the room and flew down the stairs.

I flung open the front door and leaped off the porch. Austin stared straight at me from ten feet away. I bounded at him like a football player. Without even thinking, I threw my arms around him and squeezed for all I was worth. I'd never hugged anyone as hard as I hugged my brother.

And he didn't resist. He didn't push away like he'd always done when Mom had tried to pull him close. He didn't return the hug, but he didn't struggle. I felt his heart beating against my chest, further confirmation that he was real.

I wasn't hallucinating.

My brother was back!

I couldn't even think. I was pure emotion. Relief, love, ecstatic joy, even fear overwhelmed me, churning through my brain and sending my heart into overdrive. I felt weak in the knees and had to hold on tight to keep from swooning.

We stood that way forever with the rain dribbling between us. Or maybe we only stood there a few moments. I lost track of everything. My mother's scream jarred me. I lifted my head from Austin's shoulder to find Mom and Dad standing beside the Mercedes, staring at us in open-mouthed shock.

They stumbled forward and then Mom broke into a run. She threw open her arms to embrace us, but Austin flinched from her and pressed closer to me. Mom stopped, her expression shifting from joy to hurt in a split second. Dad took her hand and pulled her in close. Her eyes filled with tears. So did his.

"Where?" That was all Dad could get out as he choked on the word.

"I looked out the window and he was here," I managed to say, my voice shaky. I hadn't realized I'd started crying too. My tears mixed with the raindrops and rolled down my cheeks.

Dad frowned as he stared at Austin. "Leslie, look at his face, his clothes."

She tilted her head and her gaze intensified. Then she gasped. "Oh, my God...he's...the same."

Dad nodded.

I kept one arm around Austin's shoulders and stepped back so I could study his face. I suddenly realized I was taller than him. That didn't make sense. He should be twenty by now. But his face... my breath froze in my lungs. His face looked the same —*exactly* the same as the day he disappeared! And his clothes... he wore the same jeans and cartoon tee!

I turned toward my astonished parents. "Dad, what's going on?"

Mom had one hand to her mouth, and then she fainted. Dad grabbed her so she didn't hit the ground. He scooped her into his arms like guys did in the movies and started up the steps to the front door. "Colton, bring Austin inside."

He watched from the porch as I stepped away from my brother, but not too far. I wanted to be close enough in case he tried to run. No way would I lose him again. I offered my hand. He stared at it a long moment and I was sure he wouldn't touch it. I glanced back at Dad and felt wet fingers slip in between mine. I turned to find Austin grasping my hand, something else he'd never done before. I gently tugged and he followed.

Dad laid Mom down on the living room couch and got her some water. Austin and I stood in the foyer, where I tried not to stare at the miracle of my unchanged brother. But he didn't seem to mind. He acted oblivious to everything, just like he'd always done. I was on a roller coaster of emotions and almost couldn't believe this was happening!

When Mom revived, she hurried to us, but Austin pressed closer to me, and she stopped. Her wide eyes brimmed with equal parts love and pain, but she smiled, looking happier than I'd seen her in the last five years.

By this time, Dad had called the police.

And once again my family lost its privacy.

Only this time it was worse.

Much worse.

So many cops showed up you'd have thought my house was under attack. Paramedics arrived, too. Dad went upstairs with Austin and me so we could change our wet clothes. None of us wanted to let Austin out of our sight. I stripped off my shirt and pants and pulled on some clean pants and a tee, while Dad took Austin to his room and tried to help him change into something dry. But Austin wouldn't cooperate.

When I entered the room, my thick hair frizzed out and damp, Dad stood with a clean shirt in hand, looking frustrated. Austin hurried to my side and waited. Dad wore the same look of rejection I'd seen on Mom's face as he shoved the shirt into my hands and left the room. Austin let me dress him.

He huddled close to me once I got him downstairs. People surrounded us and gawked. The sheriff's face looked comical when he saw my brother. The whole time-warp aspect of his appearance freaked out everyone.

The paramedics gave Austin a quick checkup, which he didn't resist. That was odd given how much he'd hated checkups in the past. Finally able to think more clearly, I studied my brother while they examined him. He never looked at the guys once. His gaze remained fixed on me, as though I was the anchor he needed. I felt guilty all over again for the harsh words I'd shouted at him five years before.

The sheriff and Detective Carter both told my parents they should get Austin to his doctor as soon as possible for a full examination. They were mystified by his appearance, especially when the paramedics said his vital signs were normal.

Mom had recovered from her initial shock and entered full-on "Mom" mode, which meant protecting Austin at all costs. The police searched the surrounding area for any signs that someone had dropped him off and by the time they'd finished, the media had arrived.

Vans crowded every bit of parking space, cameras waved in all directions, and reporters swarmed around the front entrance, but Mom refused to let any of them in.

One lady with a San Francisco TV station asked to talk with Dad outside and I took Austin to his room to keep him away from all the prying eyes.

He immediately went to the window. It was dark by then, but he stared out at the woods beyond as though he could see the trees with clarity. I knew I might not get another chance to be alone with him any time soon, so I approached. Our faces looked back at us from the glass, almost like the mirror on the adjoining wall. I was at least a foot taller. My hair had grown out and, because it was wet, stuck out in all directions like Goku in *Dragonball* Z. That's who Casey always compared me to when we went swimming together.

Austin's hair looked the same and displayed a similar Goku look, only shorter. We'd always had the spiky-wet-hair thing in common. I was still pretty lean but had filled out since Austin vanished. He was broad-shouldered, just like he'd always been. I can't really describe how it felt to stand beside the big brother everyone had written off for dead and suspect that I might now be *older* than him. I shivered and felt that weak sensation to the knees again. I placed one hand on the windowsill for support.

"Austin...do you remember the day you...disappeared?" My voice shook and I fought to control it.

What was I doing? He couldn't answer me.

"Austin, what I said to you that day, I didn't mean it, okay? I was mad. I hope you can forgive me."

Then Austin did something he'd done only once before—he turned his head and made eye contact with me.

Direct eye contact.

As though he understood me.

Uncertainly, I reached out with one trembling hand and placed it gently on his shoulder. He didn't fling it off. He stared a moment longer into my eyes and then returned his gaze to the darkened woods outside.

The next few days were insane. That's the only word to describe them. None of us wanted to be far away from Austin, so Dad worked from home, and I went on independent study. Looking back, those days after Austin's return were some of our strongest as a family.

First order of business the following morning was getting Austin to his pediatrician, who'd treated him since birth. Getting out of the house with microphones stuck in our faces and questions thrown at us like machine gun fire, *that* was tricky. Media vans and personnel camped out just beyond our driveway. Guys with photo and video cameras crawled around like cockroaches, snapping pictures of the house, the grounds, and any of us who stepped outside.

Thankfully, without permission, they couldn't "legally" enter our property. That didn't stop some Lois Lane-wannabes from sneaking around *behind* the house hoping to catch sight of

Austin or me. We were the prime targets, of course, and that made sense. Austin had come back from some kind of time warp, and I was suddenly not the child murderer I'd been labeled. Austin and I wore big hoodies that covered our faces, but I still felt like a lab rat with all those reporters ogling me like mad scientists. I hated the feeling, but Austin didn't react at all.

Once we were in the car and on our way, I thought about those rabid media people and how they liked to stir things up. They'd created the whole "Did he or didn't he murder his brother?" thing about a traumatized twelve-year-old without giving it a second thought. I guess they just thought my pain made for a good story. And now we were back in the spotlight, Austin and me. He stared out the window and I watched him, wondering if we'd ever know what really happened.

Dr. Loftus performed every test in the book on my brother. I'd never seen so much medical equipment. At first, Austin wouldn't cooperate. He didn't do the choking bird screech again —for which I was grateful—but he refused to be tested unless I was right next to him. He grabbed my hand and held on like his life depended on it. Seriously, Austin had a power-lifter grip and latched on to me like a Pitbull.

There were CT scans, an MRI of his brain, blood tests, bone density exams. You name it, his doctor had it done. Austin had to be inside a big-ass tube for the MRI and, of course, he resisted going in there.

"It'll be okay, Austin," I told him, keeping my voice steady.

"I'll be standing right outside the whole time and the noises are just the machine doing its thing."

He gave no indication he was listening, but he allowed me to lay him onto the table. I held his hand while the doctor strapped him down.

That test took almost thirty minutes, but Austin never squeezed the little bulb they gave him to indicate he wanted out. I stood in the adjoining room, which was the closest I could be to the machine, and squirmed beneath Mom's piercing gaze. She looked super pissed off and I didn't understand why. What had I done wrong this time? Even Dad gave me funny looks, like he was angry, too. I was afraid to ask, so I kept my gaze fixed on the machine.

Normally, the test results take longer to acquire but given the unusual nature of Austin's case and the involvement of law enforcement, the turnaround time for everything would only be twenty-four hours.

Dr. Loftus, an older man with gray hair and wire-rim glasses, offered us a huge smile. "From what I can see so far, Austin is perfectly healthy and that's the most important thing right now." He cast a quick sideways look at Austin, who hovered at the window gazing out into the parking lot. "Let's see what the tests tell us. Go home and enjoy having him back."

Mom nodded and we departed in silence.

Neither Mom nor Dad spoke on the drive home. Maybe it was just stress, but I felt certain they were mad at me. I dug through the details of the past few days like an archaeologist but couldn't come up with anything I'd done wrong. School was on autopilot, I hadn't gotten snarky with either of them, and I'd even cleaned up my room this week. I sat slumped in the back seat of the car beside Austin, who stared out the window, and felt once again like that troubled kid who never did anything right.

I wanted to know what crime I'd committed, but I also *didn't* want to know. I'd thought Mom was pretty much over my "failure to watch Austin closely" resentment, but maybe not. Maybe his return and, mainly, his looking the same, brought all that old anger to the surface. For Dad, too. Whatever their reasons, they were back to making me feel like gum you scrape off your shoe.

That night passed quietly once we settled in at the house. I took Austin up to his room to help him into his pajamas. Mom and Dad watched us ascend the stairs, their eyes narrowed with what I still saw as anger, but they said nothing.

Casey had come over right after we got back and when he saw Austin, he stood like an open-mouthed statue, glassy-eyed with wonder. Like me, Casey had grown a lot taller since we were twelve. Back then, Austin had been taller than both of us. Now Casey was taller than me, but Austin hadn't grown at all. I was already pretty sure he hadn't aged much more than a day.

How could that have happened?

Casey asked me that very question, and other than alien abduction, I had no answer. We were in Austin's room because I didn't want to leave my brother alone. At first, Austin stood at the window like always. I told him we needed to keep the curtains closed because guys with high-powered cameras wanted to snap his picture. Some already had when we weren't looking, and those images had been splashed all over the news and the internet like graffiti. Austin seemed to understand me and stopped pushing the drapes aside.

Keilani and Emily had blown up Discord the entire day trying to reach me, but I'd had my phone off. When Casey came over, I brought my laptop into Austin's room and set it on his bed.

Casey and I sat next to each other on the floor, while Austin drew pictures at his art table. It was almost seven my time and I was wiped. Mom was probably throwing together something for dinner, so I knew we didn't have much time. I also knew with Casey being there, neither parent would act mad at me, at least until he went home. Stifling a yawn, I clicked on the camera icon and Keilani appeared.

Her long hair was wet, and she wore a swimsuit and looked to be on her phone. I saw the beach behind her and other kids carrying surfboards.

"Oh, my God, Colton, are you alright?" She'd already talked to Casey during the day, so I knew she was talking about Austin's homecoming.

She sounded so happy to see me I almost blushed, especially with Casey sitting right there.

"Uh, yeah, I'm great, actually." I turned the computer a bit so she could see Austin at his coloring table. "There's Austin."

She leaned in more closely. Having seen his picture plenty of times, she blurted, "I can't believe it! He looks just like he did before."

I nodded.

"I'm seriously freaking out here," Casey said, his voice sounding almost breathless.

"I wish I could be there with you." She offered such an encouraging smile that Casey groaned.

"I wish you could, too," he whispered.

"Do you really think it was aliens after all, Colton?" A strong wind was blowing on the beach and Keilani kept brushing away the wet strands of hair whipping across her face.

"I don't know. We'll get the medical tests back tomorrow. Maybe there's some weird disease he got or something."

"I've gotta get back in the water in a sec. Team practice." She paused, as though afraid to say anything more. "Do you still have that picture of Kumaka I sent your dad?"

I nodded. "I printed it out and kept it with Austin's drawings. Why?"

She bit her lip and looked like she might cry. "Could you show it to Austin? I know he can't talk, but maybe he might react or something?"

I felt my emotions swell and tears burned my eyes. She looked so desperate that I felt terrible for thinking she'd given up on her brother. She'd just had to make a choice: move on with life or go psycho like me.

"Course."

I glanced at Casey and saw the same needy look on his face that I saw on Keilani's. I think maybe he felt her pain like it was his own. I crawled to the night table beside Austin's bed and slid open the top drawer. All his artwork lay within. I pulled out the stack and rifled through until I found the printout of Kumaka. My heart lurched at the young, innocent face with jet black hair and the same unemotional eyes as my brother. I returned to the computer and held it up to Keilani.

"I'm gonna show him now. Can you see his face?"

She nodded, still biting her lower lip.

I slid along the floor to Austin's worktable. Casey stayed where he was, watching with nervous anticipation.

Making sure I didn't block Keilani's line of sight, I said, "Hey, Austin."

He didn't respond. I glanced down and saw him creating yet another forest scene with a rainbow hovering overhead. Something else that hadn't changed.

"Austin, I need you to look at me."

He kept drawing.

I glanced back at Casey and then at the computer. "If I force him, he might start screaming."

Casey's eyes went wide, and I turned to look at Austin.

He was staring straight at me, just like he had last night.

I knew I might not get another chance, so I held up the picture. "Have you seen this boy before? His name is Kumaka."

I don't know what I expected, since Austin's facial expression had never really changed much during his whole life. He stared at the image but gave no indication it meant anything at all to him.

I faced Keilani. "I'm sorry."

She cried out in surprise.

I felt the picture tugged from between my fingers. I whipped my head around to find Austin holding the image and gazing at it with intensity. I watched my brother for even the slightest reaction. But he just stared long and hard at the young boy's face in his hands. Then he looked up at me and made eye contact.

I wanted to scream with frustration at not being able to understand him. I kept thinking about Alysse's claim that aliens communicate telepathically. But I only had words and those didn't work with him.

"Do you know Kumaka, Austin?"

Of course, he didn't answer. But he set the image down on his table next to the one he was drawing and resumed his artistry.

Uncertainly, I reached for the printout of Kumaka. Without even looking up, Austin causally slid his arm over the image. His message was clear. This is mine. Don't touch.

I heard Keilani make a kind of gurgling sound and turned to find Casey right up at the screen.

"Don't cry, Keilani," he assured her in a surprisingly gentle voice.

Tears slid down her cheeks. "He does know him."

Trying to not get her hopes up, I suggested, "We don't know that for sure."

She looked at me with red, teary eyes. "He does. I can tell."

I heard a voice shouting off-camera, "Hey, Keilani, we need you out here!"

She raised one hand and brushed away her tears. I thought Casey would shove his head right into the screen; he so badly wanted to comfort her.

I did, too. "I'll keep talking with him, Keilani," I assured her. "Maybe he'll draw something that's a clue. Don't give up hope."

"Don't," Casey echoed. "Kumaka will turn up, just like Austin."

She offered a strained smile. "Thanks, guys. No one else understands. I don't know what I'd do without you."

"Keilani!" That voice again, more strident this time.

She frowned. "Gotta go. Let me know everything."

"Bye, Keilani," Casey blurted.

But she was already gone, the Discord menu replacing her distraught face.

Casey and I locked eyes, and I think we both felt the same way—bad for her, but hopeful, too.

"You think Austin knows him, don't you?"

I nodded.

"So where is he?"

"Wish I knew."

We contacted Emily and she repeated the alien abduction scenario, especially given Austin's physical appearance.

"And the other kid is probably still on board their ship," she added, breathless with excitement.

"You sound so sure," Casey said flatly.

She gave him one of those haughty looks she excelled at. "Oh, Cute Boy, who's the multiple abductee here?"

Casey cracked a smile.

Alysse came on and they studied Austin as he created another mini-masterpiece.

"We'd love to come over and meet him," Alysse suggested. She sounded excited, too. "Once everything settles down, of course."

I recalled the moment at their house when they'd been staring so intently at me. "You can tell if he's been abducted, can't you?"

"Almost certainly."

"Just like we could with you, Colton," Emily added smugly.

"I'll ask Mom when would be the best time."

If she's still talking to me, that is.

But I didn't say that.

"Time for dinner!" That was Dad shouting up the stairs.

"Gotta go," I said. "We'll keep in touch."

Emily frowned. "This is only the beginning, Colton."

I froze. "Of what?"

"Of hell," she replied and ended the call.

I glanced at Casey with trepidation. He shrugged, obviously not knowing what Emily meant.

I didn't, either, until the following day when Austin's test results came back.

Chapter 8

Do You Think They Might Come Back for Him?

The next morning, I got Austin ready after he refused to let Mom help him dress. I was in my bathroom brushing my teeth when Mom barged in with a shirt and pants in her hands. I was shirtless and felt kind of weird with her just charging in like she did, but the angry look on her face cut off any snarky comment I might have made. She tossed the clothes onto the counter next to my sink like they carried smallpox.

"He doesn't want my help anymore." Her tone was sharp, her pinched face both angry and hurt. Before I could even spit out the toothpaste in my mouth, she stormed out and I heard her loud footfalls tromping down the stairs.

Eyeing Austin's haphazardly tossed clothes, it hit me that Mom was mad because Austin wanted me, not her, to help him. Was that why Dad was acting this way, too? How was it my fault that Austin refused their help? Feeling angry and resentful, I snatched up Austin's clothes and went into his room to help him get dressed.

As he pulled on his shirt, I said, "I think Mom and Dad need you to let them do stuff for you, instead of me all the time. They're *both* gonna hate me if you don't."

Of course, he said nothing.

The ride to Marin General Hospital felt so awkward I wanted to jump out the window. No one spoke. Dad focused on driving and Mom stared straight ahead like she was hypnotized. Dad had acknowledged me with a pat on the shoulder as I opened the door for Austin, and that was something, at least. Mom didn't even look in my direction.

We sat in Dr. Loftus's office and listened while he went through every one of Austin's tests. Loftus was pretty cool for a doctor. He'd been my pediatrician, too. He used to hand me a stuffed dog named Charlemagne whenever I had to get a shot and then, right before he stuck me, he'd say, "Close your eyes, Colton, and pretend Charlemagne is getting the shot." By the time I'd done that and imagined it in my mind, the shot was over.

Today Loftus looked like he'd seen a ghost because all of Austin's tests had come back... normal.

I think my mouth dropped open because Austin's condition was *anything* but normal.

"How can he look the same?" Mom's voice was fraught with fear. "Is it delayed puberty or something?"

"No, Leslie. Austin *should* be twenty years old. We know that. But I've compared our tests to the last physical we gave him shortly before his disappearance."

86

He stopped, as though he couldn't bring himself to say more.

"And?"

That was Dad. He held Mom's hand and looked older and grayer in the hair than he had just last week.

"The blood work, the brain scans, the X-Rays of his legs and arms, measurements of his feet and hands, well...I don't understand how, but Austin is *still* fifteen years old. I don't think he aged more than a few days while he was gone."

We sat there in stunned silence. It was like a science fiction movie where some dude is placed into a cryotube and frozen for five years. They wake him up and presto, he hasn't aged.

Could that have happened to Austin?

I cleared my throat, and everyone looked at me.

"Yes, Colton?" Loftus asked with a raise of his graying eyebrows.

I glanced at my parents, but quickly looked away. "You, uh, didn't, like, find any...implants in him, did you?"

Loftus looked confused. "Implants?"

I squirmed. "Yeah, like metal pieces behind his ears or in his hands or feet?"

Loftus eyed Mom and Dad a moment. Dad was about to speak, but then the doctor's eyes widened with understanding. "Oh, I see. You're thinking of those alien abduction rumors?"

I nodded. My tongue had gone dry, and I really needed some water.

"Rest assured, Colton, there is no metal in your brother's body."

My heart lurched. With happiness or disappointment, I couldn't say. "You're sure?"

"Positive. I checked for any incisions on his body before we did the tests. You may have noticed me examining behind his ears. Trying to cover all the bases, as they say. There's no metal in him. If there had been, we couldn't have conducted the MRI."

Mom sighed audibly, sagging with relief. Dad pulled her in more closely.

"That's good news, right, Colton?" Dad looked at me and I nodded. He didn't act angry now—only relieved.

Loftus's large window overlooked the parking lot. When we entered the hospital, there had been cloud cover hiding the sun. The clouds must have shifted, because all of a sudden bright sunlight poured into the office, illuminating coffee stains on the doctor's hardwood desk and casting the white windowsill in shimmering colors, almost like the window glass had become a prism.

Austin whipped his head around to gaze wide-eyed at the mini-rainbow dancing on the white sill. He hurried around the desk.

All of us watched my brother's odd behavior.

He looked out the window for only a moment before dropping to his knees and pressing his left ear up against the windowsill. I glanced at Dad, but his gaze was fixed on my brother. I watched Austin to see what he would do, but he didn't move—just kept his ear pressed against the sill. The prismatic colors danced across his face, but he took no notice.

"What's he doing?" Mom asked, a tremble evident in her voice.

"I have no idea." That was Loftus, but I didn't glance in their direction.

"You ever see him do this before, Colton?" Dad asked.

I shook my head. I realized that my heart had begun hammering with fear because Austin's behavior was beyond weird. I stepped around the desk and stopped at his side. I was afraid to touch him, so I bent down to see what he was looking at.

The parking lot was empty. The windowsill had some dust on it and there was a dead, shriveled fly in the very corner of the window. Other than that, there was nothing.

"You okay, Austin?" He acted like I wasn't there. "What are you looking at?"

Still no response of any kind. The light vanished. I looked out the window in fear, but it was only clouds drifting in front of the sun. With the light gone, the colors vanished. Austin rose to his feet and looked me right in the eye, just like he had the other night. Then he walked past me around the desk and back to his chair. He sat down as though nothing creepy had happened.

I studied Loftus and my parents. They all seemed spooked. Hell, I was, too.

"What do you make of that behavior, Doctor?" Dad asked, his voice unsteady.

The doctor removed his glasses and rubbed the bridge of his nose tiredly. After slipping the glasses back on, he eyed my parents uncertainly. "I honestly have no idea. Austin always liked rainbows and maybe the colors on the windowsill reminded him of one. I suggest keeping a close eye on him for other anomalous behaviors—anything unusual for him, that is— and report them to me at once."

Mom nodded, but her gaze was fixed on Austin, who sat straight up in his chair and gave no notice of anything.

Dad glanced at me. "You're with him the most, Colton, so let us know if he does something like that again."

He had a tone in his voice that suggested I might not tell them, like I'd hide something from him and Mom.

I nodded.

"Tom, Leslie, I don't want you to panic," Loftus went on, "but the Centers for Disease Control contacted me. They want to see all of Austin's test results."

"Why?" Dad had been leaning forward in his chair, but now he sat up.

"Because his condition is so unusual," Loftus replied evenly. I could tell he was keeping his tone low-key, even though he didn't look all that calm. "We don't know where he's been and now he comes back like...well, like he is. They want to make certain he didn't contract some heretofore unknown virus that's kept him young but might also be contagious."

"What kind of virus could keep him young?" Mom asked incredulously.

"And you just said his test results came back normal," Dad insisted.

"He is normal. Trust me on that. We found no signs of anything irregular. But they want to double-check our findings. That's all."

Mom and Dad exchanged an uncertain look between them.

"Don't they need our permission?" Dad asked.

"No."

"But Austin is a minor," Mom blurted angrily.

"Legally, Leslie, Austin is twenty years old. We have a birth certificate to prove it. As a courtesy, I'm letting you know that I must forward his test results today." He placed one hand on Mom's forearm. "I'm sure they'll find nothing, just like we didn't, but it's best to cover every angle."

Mom wasn't thrilled. That was written all over her face. But she nodded and that ended the conversation.

Headlines like "Ageless Kid Returns" and "Why Hasn't Austin Bowman Aged?" or even "Was Austin Abducted by Aliens?" soon appeared on every newsfeed and TV news outlet.

I guess if it had been someone else's brother, I'd have been interested in the story, too. But this was *my* brother and *my* family, and I resented the fact that we couldn't have privacy to deal with the mystery on our own. I got so mad that I cursed out the reporters camping in front of our house while Mom hustled Austin inside with a coat over his head. Dad grabbed me and led me in after them. The footage of me with half my words bleeped out made the news twenty-four seven for the next two days and rejuvenated my Psycho Boy status with the locals.

And Austin wasn't Austin anymore. Within a day of his return—thanks to the media—Austin became "The Ageless Kid," and neighbors pooled near our driveway hoping to catch a glimpse of him.

Our home phone rang so much, Dad finally turned it off and let everything go to voice mail. Every conceivable news outlet asked for statements and interviews and pictures of Austin—then and now. There had been plenty "then" pictures on the Net back when he went missing and, despite Mom's best efforts, there were quite a few "Now" ones showing up too. News people and paparazzi snapped photos endlessly, from close or far away, whenever we stepped outside the house.

Suddenly, Austin became his own version of those before and after weight loss ads. What really pissed me off was how people turned that image into one meme after another. Some were harmless, I admit, like the one that had the "Now" Austin pale and glittery like a *Twilight* vampire. Others were seriously nasty, and I won't even go into what they said because my blood boiled just thinking of them.

I'll give my parents major kudos for not wanting to be famous. I know there are parents out there who, if they had a miracle kid like Austin, would exploit the hell out of him. We got invited onto every chat show in existence, but my folks turned them all down. There was so much BS out there about what diseases Austin might be carrying that Dad spoke to the news media and explained that the medical tests had all come back normal. The CDC in Atlanta also poured over his test results and, within a day, officially proclaimed him "contagion free." How thoughtful of them. It was so nice to hear my brother wasn't going to start a zombie apocalypse.

The alien abduction theory kept flitting around in my head. Of all the possibilities, that one still seemed the most reasonable, despite the lack of implants. Aliens had snatched Austin when he ran into the woods, kept him somewhere for five years, and then dropped him off like they were running a carpool. Why hadn't he aged? Alien technology looked like the only answer.

I shared these thoughts with Dad a few days after Austin's return, because he no longer acted mad at me. I found him in his office on the computer.

"I've thought the same thing, Colton, but your mother wants to accept that no implants means no aliens. She can't handle even the thought that they might come back for him, so it's better to deny the possibility."

That made sense, I guess, in a *the truth is too painful, so let's hide from it* kind of way. I decided to push a little more.

"Are you still mad at me, Dad?"

He looked momentarily surprised, and then seemed to understand what I was talking about. "You mean the other night?"

I nodded.

"I wasn't mad at you, son."

"Could've fool me," I grumbled.

He caught my tone and looked slightly abashed. "Okay, I was frustrated because Austin wouldn't let me help him with anything, not that I dressed him all that often before, but still, I felt rejected. But mostly, I felt bad for your mother. She did everything for him growing up and now he comes back and flat out rejects her."

"In favor of me," I mumbled, "the son she hates for letting him wander off in the first place." Of course, my parents still didn't know what really happened that dark day.

"Colton—"

"And now she hates me all over again because Austin only wants my help and not hers. How is that *my* fault, Dad?"

"It's not, son," he said with assurance. "And you're being a typical hyperbolic teenager."

"Hyper what?" I hated it when he used words I didn't know.

"It means you're exaggerating. Your mother doesn't hate you. She never has."

My temper rose and I had to fight to keep my voice steady. "What do you call the silent treatment? The looks she gives me?"

He must have seen the storm clouds in my eyes because he placed a hand on my shoulder. "She...resents you because Austin chose you over her."

Resents? How was that better than hate?

"It's not my fault, Dad!"

He pulled back his hand and deflated slightly, looking like he aged ten years in the last ten seconds.

"Your mom loved doing things for Austin, so don't get me wrong when I say she was ecstatic—that's the best word to describe her—when you turned out to be, well, you know, not 'different'."

I nodded and listened. Dad had never opened up like this before.

"You and I, well, we always got along fine, I think, even when you, well..."

"Got a rep as a bad kid?"

He nodded this time. "But your mom, she wanted to do more for you too, you know, take care of you like mothers do. But you were so independent and stubborn, it exasperated her. So, she put everything into Austin, who never hugged her or told her he loved her. You didn't do much of that either, Colton."

I froze where I stood. Was that true? Had I always given Mom a hard time? When was the last time I told her I loved her? I honestly couldn't remember.

"Now Austin is back and shutting her out and..."

He didn't finish, but I knew the punch line. "And she's taking it out on me, like before."

"No, son. She just needs time to adjust to everything that's happened."

I didn't fully believe that but didn't say so. He'd just accuse me of being "hyperbolic" again. I decided to change the subject so my anger could cool. "I still think we should invite Emily and Alysse over to check out Austin, just in case."

Dad looked weary. "I agree. No stone unturned, as they say, and I convinced your mom it was necessary. For closure. They're coming over tomorrow for dinner. Didn't Emily tell you?"

I shook my head. I hadn't been on Discord with Emily all day.

Dad leaned back in his desk chair and studied me. "You've really been great with Austin since his return, son. I thank you for that, even if your mom can't just yet."

Embarrassed, I felt my face heat up. I wasn't used to compliments. "He's my brother."

Dad shifted his position. "I've been thinking about what Alysse told us." He paused, and I waited expectantly. "If aliens *are* the reason Austin vanished, do you think they might come back for him?"

"I don't know."

But from that day on, I slept on Austin's floor in a sleeping bag. No one would take him again without a fight.

I contacted Emily from my laptop to talk about their impending visit. I didn't add Casey and Keilani to the chat because I just wanted to scope out Emily's thoughts. I filled her

in on the negative test results and she just shrugged noncha-
lantly, like always. Nothing seemed to ruffle her self-assured
feathers—at least nothing I'd ever seen.

"No implants doesn't mean no aliens, Psycho Boy," she
stated as though it were a fact and not her opinion. "Lots of
abductees don't have them."

"Do you think you and your mom will be able to tell from
his aura?"

Her face shifted into that smug self-confidence she always
wore when discussing this topic. "Of course. Does he still look
at everything through mirrors?"

I lurched in my chair. I'd forgotten about the mirrors. We'd
taken them all down over the years, except the one in Austin's
room, but he didn't seem to mind their absence.

"No. I didn't even realize that until you just mentioned it.
What could it mean?"

She shrugged. "Beats me. That hasn't been part of abductee
mythology."

"My mom doesn't believe in the abduction possibility
anymore, not since Dr. Loftus told her about no implants."

She laughed. "Your mom's a fool."

I guess she thought I'd agree or something, but anger welled
up within me and I leaned closer to the screen. "Watch your
mouth! That's my mom you're talking about!"

She looked surprised. "Whoa, slow down, Psycho Boy.
You're the one who always talks smack about her, how she hates
you and treats you badly. You said it again last night."

It was true, I had said that. But only out of frustrated anger.
"Doesn't matter. My mom's not a fool, so shut your mouth. I'm
outta here!"

I closed Discord and Emily whooshed away into cyber-space. I sat back in my desk chair, breathing hard. I didn't care who was doing it, I couldn't let anyone diss my family.

Discord popped back up with an incoming call. It was Emily. I closed it again and the chirping ring ceased. I stared at the screen, but she didn't call back.

Why had I gotten so mad? Maybe because I thought Emily might be sort-of right? Maybe it *was* foolish of Mom to dismiss the alien possibility just because there was no physical evidence. But that didn't give Emily the right to call her names.

The Discord "ring" blasted out again and I almost jumped. It was Keilani this time. Emily must've called her. I clicked on her icon and Keilani appeared on screen. She was in her room, at her desk, because I could see the bed behind her with all Kumaka's stuffed animals lining the headboard. She'd told us that keeping them made her feel close to him.

"Are you okay, Colton?" she asked. "Emily just called and said you went psycho on her."

Leave it to Em to go hyperbolic. "I didn't go psycho on her. She called my mom a fool and I got mad and hung up. End of story."

I sounded testy and felt bad when she cringed at my tone. "Okay, but you sound pretty mad now and I didn't do anything."

Remorse flooded over me, and I let go of my anger. "Sorry. But she had no right to say that."

"True, but you know how she is."

I nodded. We all knew how abrasive Emily could be.

Keilani brushed her black hair back over her shoulder and

seemed to study my face. "Maybe because you sometimes talk smack about your mom, Emily thought you didn't love her."

I flinched. Was that how I sounded when I was mad at my mom? "Of course, I love my mom, Keilani," I said quietly, and then paused. "I just wish she loved *me*."

Her pretty face dissolved into one of deep empathy. "Oh, Colton, I'm sorry."

I felt the beginnings of tears and fought them off. "I gotta go. Talk tomorrow?"

She offered a genuine smile. "Of course. It's the best part of my day."

That made me feel a bit better and we ended the call.

I thought about the whole mirror thing. Since returning, Austin had spent most of his time focusing on me or on drawing new works of art, none of which depicted spaceships or weird creatures, either. Despite his outward appearance not changing, something within him clearly did. What could it all mean?

My ringing cell interrupted my thoughts. I glanced at the screen. Emily. I ignored it. I had brushed away those tears and didn't want to be upset any more that night. The call went to voice mail. I saw the voice mail icon and considered deleting it without listening but decided that would be unfair. I swiped open my phone and pressed the voice mail button and the word *speaker* next to it.

Emily's voice poured forth. "I'm sorry, Colton, for insulting your mom. I know how I feel when people do that to me. I'm, well, kind of my own worst enemy and have a big mouth. I'm sorry."

The little slider reached the end of the message and stopped. She'd called me "Colton." When was the last time she'd done that? The first day we met at her house three and a half years ago? I think she really *was* sorry. Like me with my temper, she knew her mouth ran away with her brain far too often.

I opened a text window. I really didn't want to talk any more that night. Between the dad conversation and this one, my emotions were thrashed. I typed in: *Apology accepted.*

She typed: *Can I still come tomorrow with my mom?*

I considered only a moment. She was my friend. Friends made things right with each other, just like Casey made it right with me when we were twelve.

I typed: *You better or else.*

I got the vomiting emoji in reply.

Em was still Em.

The following morning, I brought Austin down to the kitchen after helping him shower. I must admit, having to help my fifteen-year-old (well, twenty, if you want to be accurate) brother shower was kind of weird. I'd never helped him with that stuff before and those first few days were awkward. I guess it was because I kept recalling the nasty assertions about Austin and me doing "stuff" with each other that made me feel like a pervert for watching him in the shower. But someone had to be there in case he slipped or turned on the water too hot or whatever, and I was his designated choice.

Getting him breakfast was easy because we both ate cereal. Austin wore a tee shirt and shorts and strode across our enormous kitchen to sit in his usual seat at the table. As I headed for the cereal cupboard, I noticed the phone light flashing. Like I said, Dad had turned off the ringer, but the light meant an incoming call. Not sure why, I stepped over and picked up the handset, switching it to speaker mode.

"Hello?"

"Hello" came a pleasant male voice. "I'm Anderson Cooper and I'd like to speak with Mr. or Mrs. Bowman."

My eyes bugged out. I knew this guy. I'd seen him on television, mainly back when Austin first vanished.

"The CNN dude?" I asked, suddenly thinking it could be a prank.

A chuckle wafted out of the speaker. "The very same. And you must be Colton."

I stiffened. "How'd you know?" I pictured cameras spying on me through the kitchen windows and glanced around nervously.

"I don't think your father would refer to me as 'the CNN dude,'" came the reply, followed by another chuckle.

I relaxed. "Uh, sorry. What can I do for you?" I was trying to be on my best behavior after my meltdown the other day.

"I'd love the opportunity to interview you and your parents. At your home, of course. I'd set everything up."

"Why?" It was a dumb question, but it slipped out anyway.

Cooper didn't tell me it was a dumb question. "The whole world is interested in how your family is coping. Especially you, Colton."

"Me?"

"Your efforts to locate Austin these past five years have been extraordinary, above and beyond what most brothers would do."

"How do you know so much about me?"

"Local sources. You know how people love to gossip."

I bristled. "Yeah, so don't believe everything you hear."

"The trouble is, Colton, people do believe what they hear. That's why I want to get you and your family on record to talk truth, not rumor."

I considered for a moment. It sounded like a good idea. I could finally tell my story and maybe ditch my Psycho Boy rep for good.

"Mom'll never let Austin on camera."

"That's fine." I could almost see him shrug. I pictured that silver hair and him looking calm like he always does on TV. "You and your parents. A chance to tell your story the way you want it to be told."

I paused and glanced across the kitchen at Austin. He stared back, almost like he was listening.

"Okay," I finally said. "I'll see if my parents'll go for it."

"Excellent. Here's my cell number. Have them call me and we'll set everything up." He rattled off a number that I scribbled onto the pad by the phone.

"Thanks, Mr. Cooper," I said, and meant it. He seemed like a cool guy, at least over the phone.

"I like 'CNN dude' better," he replied.

I laughed. "Later, CNN dude."

There was a click, and I replaced the handset in its cradle. Then I set about preparing breakfast.

At first Mom said, "Not a chance," when I mentioned Anderson Cooper's call, and Dad backed her up.

I hesitated before going on. This CNN thing had given me an idea, a way to do what Dr. Bernstein had been saying I should do for the past five years.

"I wanna do it."

Dad studied me closely. "Why?"

I tried to hold his gaze, but embarrassment swept over me and I glanced down. "I just think it's time for me to be straight up about everything and why I been so crazy these past five years. I think that's a good place to do it because I have a feeling other kids have been where I've been and it might help them, maybe, to know they're not alone."

They both looked at me as though I'd spoken Chinese, and I couldn't blame them. It had come out kind of loony sounding, I guess.

"Please, Mom," I pleaded, knowing if she said "yes," Dad would go along. "I really wanna do this." I ignored the fact that she'd been ignoring me. This was too important.

She and Dad eyed each other. He shrugged and she turned to face me. "Austin will not be on camera. I will not exploit him."

"I already told Mr. Cooper that. His cell number is on the pad by the phone. He said call him any time and he'll set everything up."

Dad's eyes bugged out. "He gave you his cell number?"

I shrugged. "Sure, why not?"

"Maybe because he's a famous CNN journalist."

Mom looked at me with suspicion. "Why can't you just say what you want to us, without the cameras?"

"Because I can't!" I snapped. Her insinuating tone had rattled me.

"Colton." Dad eyed me and shook his head slightly so Mom wouldn't see.

She gazed at me a long moment. Then she nodded and rose to leave the family room.

Dad stood too. "I'll give him a call."

I stood and faced my father. I was now taller than him, which I hadn't noticed till that moment. He must've noticed too because he kind of shook his head in wonder.

"Thanks, Dad."

Dad and Mr. Cooper had a great talk over the phone, or so Dad told me, and they'd set up the interview for tomorrow afternoon.

My mouth dropped open in shock. "That quick? They can get all their stuff out here in one day?"

"They go where the news is, son, and they have to do it fast or they miss the 'scoop.' Right now, Austin is the scoop."

"It won't be live, will it?" Now that it was happening, I was beginning to have second thoughts.

"No. It will be edited and aired tomorrow night. That way if we mess up, they can cut it out."

I nodded, wondering if I would mess up. "Can I see Dr. Bernstein tomorrow morning, you know, before the interview?"

Dad tilted his head slightly. "Of course. But this was your idea, Colton. You *can* talk to me about whatever is on your mind."

I felt bad because I heard the hurt in his voice. Both Mom and Dad resented how easily I could talk about my feelings with Dr. Bernstein. "I know, but I really need to see her first."

Dad looked resigned. "Okay. You make the appointment. I'll drive you."

"Thanks, Dad."

Then I did something that surprised even me. I gave him a quick hug before hurrying out of his office. When was the last time I'd hugged him—when I was six or seven? I knew teens were supposed to dismiss their parents and not want them around, but I liked it when my dad offered to do things for me— like drive me to Dr. Bernstein's office, even though I had my own license.

The impending interview with Anderson Cooper should have been enough drama for one morning. But around eleven o'clock, my life got a whole lot weirder because Homeland Security paid us a visit, and it wasn't a social call.

Chapter 9

We're Here About Austin

As I was tromping down the stairs to get my water bottle from the kitchen, the doorbell rang. Mom and Dad were upstairs in their bedroom discussing tomorrow's interview—I'd heard Cooper's name mentioned as I passed by their door.

Dad called down. "Colton, can you see who's at the door? If it's reporters, our response is—"

"No comment," I called up to him. I knew the drill by now.

I strode across the foyer to the door and peered through the beveled glass panels. A man and a woman stood on the porch. They looked very ordinary, maybe in their forties, but pretty old for sure. The man had a short buzz cut and a serious, pinched face, as though he never smiled. The woman looked more relaxed. They were dressed in casual pants and polo shirts.

"Can I help you?" I said through the door.

The woman leaned closer, and I noted red hair. "Colton?

We'd like to speak with you and your parents. It's very important."

I hesitated, not sure what to do. "Uh, what about?"

I didn't recognize them, but they sure knew me. Of course, *everyone* knew me by now.

The woman glanced back toward the driveway, then stepped up close to the door. She slipped a piece of paper out of her pocket and held it up against the glass. I leaned in to read the handwritten note.

We are from Homeland Security. We need to talk,
but we don't want the media to know we're here.

Then the man pressed an official badge up against the glass. It was shaped kind of like a large body with big hips and the waist tapering in. At the top was a golden eagle and right under that, *Homeland Security Investigations*. There was also a circle with the words *U.S. Department of Homeland Security* in it. At the very bottom was a blue banner with the words *Special Agent* in gold.

I stepped back in shock. That badge looked hella official, despite the unofficial way they were dressed. I glanced at the note again.

We don't want the media to know we're here.

That could explain the casual clothes. To the media parked at the end of our driveway, these two would just look like friends of my parents.

They pulled the paper and badge back, slipping them into their pockets while I debated what to do. I decided they must be legit.

"Hey Dad, could you come down here, please?" I leaned closer to the glass and said, "I'm getting my parents."

The woman nodded. The man stared back like he could wait all day. I stepped aside as Dad and Mom descended the stairs. She looked suspicious, but then she always did these days.

"What's up, Colton?" Dad asked as they crossed the foyer.

I indicated the door with a nod of my head. "They're from Homeland Security."

Mom gasped and Dad squinted through the glass at the couple outside. "Don't look like it."

"I think it's a disguise. They don't want the media to know."

Dad frowned.

"What they said, anyway." I shrugged. This was their call.

My parents exchanged an uncertain look. Mom nodded and Dad reached for the door handle. He ushered the couple into the foyer and asked to see their identification.

This time, both agents produced identical badges and held them out. These were definitely the real deal. She introduced herself as "Special Agent Spencer" and he as "Special Agent Martin."

Mom invited them into the living room. The agents sat on the couch while my parents planted themselves on the loveseat across from them. I sank into Dad's easy chair off to the side and listened, intent on catching every word.

"How can we help you?" Dad asked, sounding fatigued. The constant barrage of media and police attention had clearly gotten to him.

"We're here about your son," Agent Martin said curtly and without inflection.

Dad and I must've been thinking the same thing because he spoke my thoughts aloud. "Colton lost his temper with the reporters the other day, Agent Martin. I know he sounded threatening, but he isn't dangerous. I can assure you of that."

Agent Spencer glanced at me. I was leaning forward with my arms on my knees and must've looked scared because she offered a smile. "Not Colton. We're here about Austin."

Mom stiffened. "Why? You deal with national security."

"That's correct," Spencer said agreeably. Martin seemed kind of detached, but she looked sympathetic. "And we feel what happened to Austin might have national security implications."

"How so?" Dad wrapped one arm around mom. "The FBI found no evidence of where he might have been taken."

"And he's not gonna start a zombie apocalypse either," I snapped without thinking. "The CDC said so." I guess everything was getting to me, too.

"Colton," Dad said in that cautionary tone he had.

"We know all that," Martin put in, his voice cool and casual. "But we have information the FBI doesn't. They deal primarily with internal threats. We are international."

"You think Austin was taken out of the country?" Dad sounded shocked, like that idea had never occurred to him. In truth, we'd never talked about that possibility, except within the alien abduction scenario. In that case Austin would have been taken out of the country for sure. Off the planet, too.

I realized my thoughts had wandered.

"...classified," Spencer was saying when I refocused on the conversation, "but we've been authorized to share enough information with you to secure your cooperation."

Mom shifted to full-on "mom" mode. "Cooperation for what?"

"To have Austin examined by our scientists."

"He's been examined already," Dad said, sounding testy.

"We know." Martin spoke this time. It was like they took turns. Kind of weird if you ask me. "But our tests are different. We're looking for something no one else knew to look for, something that could endanger you and your neighbors."

"What?"

Now it was Spencer's turn. "In this setting, that's classified. We're permitted to share limited information with you, but only at our west coast headquarters in San Francisco. And you must sign legally binding nondisclosure agreements. Austin, too."

"Austin?" Mom sat forward in surprise. "Austin doesn't talk."

Martin remained impassive. "He's legally an adult. He needs to sign."

"He doesn't know how," Dad explained.

Spencer said, "Very well. You will sign for him."

"And Colton cannot accompany us." That was Martin.

I leaped to my feet. "Now wait a minute—"

Dad held up a hand in my direction. "Calm down, son."

Feeling my chest tighten with anger, I slowly lowered myself back into the easy chair, glancing from Dad to the stoic agents.

"Why not Colton?" Dad asked, keeping his voice even. But I heard the tightness. He was starting to lose it.

"He's a minor, Mr. Bowman," Spencer said in a gentle, understanding voice that surprised me.

"And he has a reputation," Martin added dryly.

"I do not!" I was on my feet before I knew it, fists clenched.

The two agents eyed me without emotion, as though I'd

done exactly what they expected. And I guess I had. I unclenched my fists.

Dad glanced my way, but kept his attention focused on Martin and Spencer. "In that case, we'll have to say no to your tests. For reasons we don't understand, Austin only allows Colton to take care of him. I can't even help change his clothes." Mom winced and Dad took her hand gently. "If Colton doesn't go, Austin won't go."

The agents looked at one another uncertainly.

Spencer cleared her throat. "Then you give us no choice, Mr. Bowman. Colton may come. But bear this in mind—you and your wife will sign for him. If at any point, should he or you breathe a word of what you see and hear, you will be sent to federal prison. Colton will not, but you will. Is that understood?"

"Of course, it is," Dad replied, shifting uncomfortably. "We're law-abiding people here, Agent Spencer. All we want to know is what happened to our son. And for him to be safe."

Spencer nodded. "Then we're on the same page, Mr. Bowman."

Even though Mom hadn't said anything, I knew she'd been listening to every word. She had this way of squinting her eyes ever so slightly when she was concentrating on a conversation.

"Only Dr. Loftus will perform tests on Austin," she said so firmly it sounded like a door closing. "He's the only one I trust."

Spencer smiled for the first time, though her partner didn't. She had a warm smile, I realized. It filled up the lower half of her face and made her look like she could be your best friend.

"Of course, Mrs. Bowman. That's why he's outside in the car."

"What?" Mom looked stunned. So did Dad.

"We cleared his schedule and picked him up on our way over," Martin offered in his monotone voice.

"You want to do this today?" Dad sounded incredulous.

I was shocked, too. It was already eleven o'clock and Alysse and Emily were scheduled for dinner.

"It could seriously be a matter of life and death, Mr. Bowman," Spencer said gravely. "The tests won't take long, and we should know the results within a day."

"Does this have anything to do with aliens?" I had to ask.

Spencer raised her eyebrows, but Martin merely stared without expression. "We cannot say more until we are in a secure environment and the appropriate documentation signed."

Mom was scared. I saw it in the way she crinkled her mouth and widened her eyes.

Dad looked scared, too. "Will these tests hurt Austin?"

"They're minimally invasive, Mr. Bowman," Spencer went on, her voice soothing and calm. I guess they decided she was the better one to talk about the "human" stuff. "We need a fresh blood sample. Then a dye will be injected into Austin's blood stream and a scan taken of his entire body. That's it."

There was a long moment of silence. We all watched Mom. Even the agents seemed to sense this was her call. I hoped she'd say yes. I really wanted to know what those tests were looking for.

"Dr. Loftus has to approve your tests once we're there," Mom said cautiously, as though still debating within her mind.

"Agreed," Spencer said with a nod.

Mom looked across at me as though wondering if I might be an alien myself.

"Okay."

That was all she said.

I went upstairs to get Austin ready.

Mom canceled the dinner plans with Alysse and Emily, telling them she'd reschedule after the Anderson Cooper interview.

Over the past five years, Dad and I had watched every *X-Files* episode and the *UFO Diaries*. Both series were about conspiracy stuff, so it didn't surprise me when he told the agents we would follow in our own car. At this point, after so many years of online searches for answers to Austin's disappearance, I'd become pretty fringy and welcomed Dad's decision.

Mom thanked Dr. Loftus for taking the day off.

"Didn't have much choice, Leslie," he said with a nod toward Agents Martin and Spencer in the front seat of their black sedan. "They cleared my schedule."

Mom looked upset. "I'm sorry."

Loftus smiled. "Don't be. I'm just as curious as you about what they're looking for."

Mom returned to our car. Dad patted her gently on the hand and started driving, following the agents' two-door sedan past the reporters and up Marin View Avenue.

Homeland Security's San Francisco office was situated on Golden Gate Avenue. The building looked to be made of concrete blocks, with twenty floors and, like, ten thousand windows. Okay, probably not that many, but a lot.

After parking in an underground garage, the agents took us upstairs in an elevator. Mom fidgeted and Dad kept his arm around her. Austin stood beside me staring at the numbers lighting up in succession as we ascended.

We exited into a carpeted hallway that looked ordinary at first glance, but some of the wooden doors had keypads rather than knobs or deadbolts. We followed the agents to one of the doors and waited while Spencer punched in a code. I couldn't see the numbers because Martin turned to face us and blocked her from view.

The door slid open, and I followed my parents into something straight out of a *Star Trek* show. No joke there. This lab was enormous, metallic, shiny, and futuristic all at the same time. Computers abounded, with screens of varying sizes, but they looked so high tech compared to what I was used to that they might as well be from another planet. Everything was touch screen, but the way people in white coats touched and swiped those screens looked · more Tony Stark than Windows 11.

A huge, curved chamber surrounded by glass filled the far end of the lab. A human-body-sized computer screen sat just outside the chamber with metal-encased cables snaking to and from the enclosure. A touch-screen panel rested beside it.

All this technology overwhelmed my senses as I followed my equally amazed parents and Dr. Loftus across the length of the lab. Austin crowded in against me and I felt bad that I'd been more focused on the equipment than him. His gaze flitted about the room nervously and I kept him as close to me as possible.

We halted before a white-haired man seated at a computer station examining charts on the screen. Martin and Spencer stopped, and the man looked up.

He had a friendly face, with lots of wrinkles that made me think he smiled more than he frowned, and a named imprinted to the left chest area of his white lab coat: Conners. His active brown eyes instantly focused on Austin.

"You brought him," the white-haired man said quietly. But there was an edge of excitement to his voice.

Martin made a tiny grunting noise that sounded to me like a "Duh." But Spencer simply introduced everyone.

"This is quite a lab you have here, Dr. Conners," Loftus said as he shook the man's hand.

"State of the art," Conners replied with a grin. But even as he thanked my parents for coming, his eyes kept drifting to Austin, as though he expected to see whatever he was looking for without the aid of his machines.

"Do you have the required paperwork, Dr. Conners?" Martin asked in his deadpan voice.

"Of course." Conners turned and slid a light panel out from the console. I leaned in for a better view and spotted what looked like a virtual document.

Dad stepped forward. "I'd like to read that, if you don't mind."

"Naturally." Conners stepped away from the panel and Dad took over the chair.

As he leaned in to read the document, Dr. Loftus asked, "What exactly are these tests you intend to perform?"

Conners glanced at the two agents.

Spencer said, "I'm afraid you all must sign the nondisclosure agreement before we can share that information. Would you like to read it, as well, Dr. Loftus?"

"No. As long as Tom and Leslie agree, so do I. Austin is their son."

"Then we await Mr. Bowman's decision." That was Martin, cool as ever.

I squirmed as his gaze locked on mine. He seemed to be looking right through me, as though everything that was about to happen revolved around me, not Austin. Maybe it did. If I told Austin not to do the tests, would he refuse? I wondered if that was what Agent Martin was thinking, though his face was devoid of expression, so I couldn't tell.

Dad looked up from the glowing panel. "How do I get a copy of this once it's signed?"

"There's a box for your email address, Mr. Bowman," Spencer explained and leaned in to scroll down with her finger.

Dad eyed her suspiciously. It was that *X-Files* look he'd developed over the past five years, the one that said, "trust no one."

She must've understood, because she bent down to the virtual keyboard. This time I stepped closer to see. She typed an email address into the box, but each time she touched a letter or character it appeared for a second and then vanished. "This is a secure server, Mr. Bowman. The document will go to you alone and we keep a copy in our system."

Dad gave Mom a long look. When she nodded, he turned

back to the panel and accepted the silver stylus Conners slipped from his pocket. Dad paused, his hand hovering above the panel. I leaned over his shoulder and spotted the words "Federal Prison" in bold letters, followed by "twenty years." My throat went dry.

Dad scrawled his signature and typed in his email, then extended the stylus to Mom.

Her fingers trembled as she took it, and Dad placed a comforting hand on her shoulder as she signed. Mom stepped back and handed the stylus to Spencer.

Spencer turned to Loftus. "Your turn, Doc."

Loftus scrawled an unreadable signature and handed back the pen. Spencer touched a button beside the panel and it slid closed, leaving no trace it had ever been there. Everyone turned to face Dr. Conners.

"Well," Loftus said, sounding all business, "What tests do you wish to perform, Dr. Connors?"

I was grateful that he stepped up because I could tell my parents were almost paralyzed with fear. So was I.

"We need a fresh blood sample. That's number one. Number two, we want to inject a harmless dye into Austin's blood stream, and then we'll have him stand in here." He led us to the curved glass chamber. "This is a scanning chamber, something like an X-Ray and MRI rolled into one. The particulars are classified, so I can't be more specific than that, but it will scan Austin's entire body and hopefully show us if what we're looking for is present. The blood work will also be used to verify its presence."

"What presence?" Loftus asked, clearly confused. "We did

every conceivable lab test. The CDC confirmed my findings. He's contagion free."

"Yes, I've seen all your findings," Conners said, his voice kind of cagey, like he was dancing around a giant elephant in the room. "But none of those tests were intended to find what we're looking for."

"And what are you looking for?" That was Dad, finally finding his voice.

Conners glanced uncertainly at Spencer.

"Let me explain as much as we're allowed, Mr. Bowman," she said. Martin gave her a look that said, *be careful.*

What were they hiding? My whole body felt as tense as a coiled spring with all this build up.

"You're fully aware, I'm sure, of terrorists who strap bombs to their person and blow themselves up in crowded venues. It happens in many parts of the world."

Mom gasped. "What does that have to do with my son?"

Spencer's face displayed genuine empathy. "Hopefully nothing, Mrs. Bowman. But imagine, if you will, a new technology that places the explosives not *outside* the body, but within it."

Dad's mouth dropped open. "That's impossible. Isn't it?"

"You think my son has a bomb inside him?" Mom's voice quavered, and it sounded like she was about to lose it.

But my mind was already two steps ahead. My five years of internet searches had taught me a lot. "You're talking about weaponized nanotechnology, aren't you?"

I said it without thinking. Conners and the agents turned to me with surprised expressions. Even Loftus looked amazed.

"You're a smart boy, Colton," Martin said flatly.

Loftus stepped toward the agents. "What are you talking about? What's 'weaponized nanotechnology'?"

"We're not talking about it. Colton is." Spencer turned to me, her expression neutral. "Please continue, Colton."

Dad and Mom stared at me in confusion. While Dad and I had talked about alien abductions, I'd never mentioned this weaponized nano thing because it didn't seem applicable to Austin's case. But maybe it was?

I tried to swallow, but I had no saliva left. "Well, uh, I read on this one website that, uh, well microscopic nanites can be created using a person's DNA and made to act like iron in the bloodstream. That way the body doesn't reject them and they don't show up on metal detectors and stuff."

My parents and Loftus looked at me with eyes the size of boiled eggs. But Spencer, Martin, and Conners could've passed for statues in a wax museum.

I glanced at my brother, because all of a sudden I was terrified. "I, uh, I guess the idea is to put a mircodrop of nitroglycerin into each nanite, which could then be detonated by remote control, or else by a built-in timer. The whole person would, like, well...explode."

Mom's hand flew to her mouth. I turned my head to find Austin staring at me. Was he trying to tell me that I'd hit on the truth? Or that I was wrong?

Loftus looked more rattled than I'd ever seen him. He stared at the silent agents with deep intensity. "Such a scenario isn't possible, is it?"

"That's classified, Dr. Loftus," Spencer offered, her voice tempered with extreme caution. "But let's just say that Colton found a very *informative* website."

Even Dad had paled by this time. "Does that technology even exist?"

"Extremists always look for every conceivable way to bring death and destruction to those they don't accept," Martin said flatly. "That's as much as we can tell you."

"So, these tests are designed to detect the presence of biologically-based nanites?" Loftus asked, his tone one of incredulity.

The agents gazed back but did not respond. Loftus turned to Conners. He wore the same poker face.

"It's not possible," Loftus finally said when no one answered.

"Then you shouldn't mind us searching for the impossible, should you, Doctor?" Conners replied smoothly. "After all, there has been no credible explanation for Austin not aging."

"How could what Colton described affect Austin's growth?"

"That's the main reason we want to run these tests, Doctor Loftus. Something has impeded his growth hormone or his pituitary gland. Despite the medical tests showing nothing anomalous, clearly something unusual affected his brain."

Loftus turned to my parents. "I say we leave now. This is science fiction."

"Science fiction is only fiction until it becomes fact, Doctor Loftus," Spencer put in calmly, as though lecturing a student.

Dad looked at Mom. It was her call, that look said. Then Mom did something that surprised me. She let go of Dad and reached out to take my hands in hers. I couldn't remember the last time she did that.

"Colton." Her voice was practically a whisper, like she had no breath left.

"Yeah, Mom?"

She looked from me to Austin and then back at me. Right at me. Into my eyes. It felt like all my troubled-kid years piling up into this one moment in time, like she needed me now more than ever before. All the resentment and past anger melted from her eyes.

"Colton, what you just said, what you read about."

"Yeah?"

"Do you think it's even remotely possible?"

My mind raced. This was all on me now. I knew in that moment she would allow the tests if I said so. I felt small and huge at the same time, and petrified. As fringy as that website had been, the ideas on it scared the hell out of me. Because they sounded plausible.

I nodded.

Mom squeezed my hands a moment before turning to Loftus. "Do the tests."

He looked surprised. "Okay, Dr. Conners, let's get started."

I stayed by Austin's side as Conners led us to another console. He touched a virtual button and a tray slid out. On it were sterile syringes and tubes for storing blood, and other medical stuff I didn't recognize.

The two docs pulled on latex gloves and Loftus prepared a syringe. Conners held up the rubber strip to tie off Austin's upper arm, looking at me for permission to do so.

Austin let me remove his jacket and I handed it to Dad. My brother wore a *Superman Bizarro* tee underneath.

"Dr. Loftus is going to take some blood, Austin," I said in a calm voice. I didn't want my fear to be obvious to him. "You know the drill."

Loftus tied the rubber strip around Austin's upper arm and

a prominent vein protruded in the crook. He took two full tubes of blood before pulling out the needle and pressing a Band-Aid over the puncture.

Austin did nothing the entire time but stare at me. He didn't even flinch when the needle stuck him. Conners prepared a syringe with a blue-colored liquid. Loftus asked Conners what was in the dye, but I didn't understand the technical ingredients. It just looked like food coloring to me.

"His urine will be blue for the next twenty-four hours," Conners said as he handed Loftus the syringe. "But that's perfectly normal."

I heard Mom react with a slight groan, but kept my gaze fixed on Austin. In went the dye without the slightest reaction from my brother. Now it was time for the chamber. Austin had never been locked in anywhere and I didn't know how he'd act once those glass doors sealed him inside.

Other than having a door that closed, the chamber looked as though it operated like the airport scanners people had to step into, except Austin wouldn't have to raise his arms over his head. I led him inside and then stepped out quickly. I stood by the open door and Austin stared at me, so I offered my best smile. "It'll be okay, Austin. You won't be in there for long."

"About ten minutes," Conners said as he pressed a virtual button on the console beside the chamber. The curved glass opening slid shut and locked my brother within.

I stepped back to give the doctors space.

"What exactly will happen?" Loftus asked, his tone one of suspicion.

Conners grunted as he punched in numbers and programmed the machine. "Nothing harmful, Dr. Loftus. Just a full body scan. He'll feel nothing. You can watch on the large screen here."

He pointed to the body-sized computer screen, and we all drifted in that direction. Something powered up, like the humming of a beehive, only more muted. Bluish light began in a kind of wave from the top of the chamber to the bottom, from Austin's head to his feet in a slow, rhythmic fashion and then moved back up.

The large screen filled with the outline of Austin's body. With each up and down pass of the blue light, I saw more of him: his bones first, then his organs, then his muscles, then his arteries and veins. I almost had to turn away. This was worse than watching Austin take a shower; I felt like I was invading every bit of his privacy. I glanced at Mom and saw her cringe. I knew she was thinking the same thing. It felt like we were parading Austin around downtown Mill Valley stark naked.

I couldn't look anymore and stepped back in front of the chamber so Austin could see me. He didn't react to the light or the buzzing sounds, but I saw him focus on me when I stepped out front. That made me feel better.

After ten minutes, Conners returned to the console and touched the screen. The wave of light cut out and the buzzing noise powered down to nothing. He touched another button and the chamber slid open. A tiny exhalation of trapped air whooshed forth.

I hurried inside and took Austin gently by the arm. He didn't resist. I helped him out so he wouldn't trip over the lip at the bottom of the entrance, and we stood before my parents.

"Could you see anything unusual during the test?" Dad asked Conners, his gaze drifting to the two agents.

Conners shook his head. "We have to study all the data, as well as examine his blood."

"When will you know?" I asked.

"In approximately twenty-four hours," Conners replied matter-of-factly, like searching for human time bombs was a daily routine.

For all I knew, it was.

"We'll contact you tomorrow," Martin said, his tone all business.

"I'll call you personally," Spencer added in a much more sympathetic voice. "Come, I'll walk you back to your car."

We shook hands with Conners and Martin, and then Spencer indicated that Austin and I should walk with her. Loftus and Dad stayed on either side of Mom. She looked a bit shaky, and I didn't blame her.

"Do you really think my brother is a human time bomb?" I hated to put it that way and heard Mom gasp behind me, but I wasn't known for subtlety.

Spencer eyed me. "Off the record, I think it's a long shot. It was Agent Martin's idea."

"He's weird."

"He's on the spectrum."

I nearly gagged. "Seriously?"

She nodded. "Not much for conversation, but superb deductive skills and excellent instincts about unusual cases like this one."

I looked at her with embarrassment. "Wow. I just thought he was weird and rude."

She offered a sympathetic smile. "Like your friends thought about Austin?"

123

I burned with shame and didn't speak again until we were in the underground garage. We had to take Loftus with us, but we'd brought the SUV, so there was room.

Dad thanked Agent Spencer for her help.

"We'll talk soon." She smiled.

He nodded and held open the passenger door for Mom. As he walked around to the driver's side and Loftus slipped into the back seat, Spencer turned to me. She extended her hand.

Confused, I shook. "What's that for?"

"For being a great brother. Your devotion to finding Austin these past five years has been inspiring."

I almost choked, especially given what I planned to say on the Anderson Cooper show tomorrow. "Uh, thanks."

"I'd stay away from those websites you mentioned, however. They are monitored. I wouldn't want you getting into trouble."

I tensed up. Monitored? "Okay. Now that Austin's back, I haven't been on them, anyway."

She studied me a moment while Mom watched us from the passenger seat. "What do *you* think happened to your brother, Colton?"

I hesitated. Did I believe the nano-bomb theory? No. "I still think it was aliens. Do you believe in alien abduction, Agent Spencer?"

Her face didn't change, but her voice lowered. "Officially, no." I gazed at her, waiting for more. But she just smiled. "Good luck on Anderson Cooper tomorrow."

I froze. "How'd you know about that?" I pictured my house under surveillance by Homeland Security.

She chuckled. "CNN has been running promos all day. Saw one on my phone driving over here."

I grinned with relief. "Thanks, Agent Spencer. And I'm sorry for what I said about Agent Martin."

"Not to worry. He's used to it."

But he shouldn't have to be, I thought, as I eased Austin into the back seat beside Loftus and then slid in beside him. *No one should.*

Chapter 10

Colton, What's that Drawing?

No one spoke on the way home. It was midafternoon, so there was a ton of traffic crossing the Golden Gate Bridge and jamming the 101 freeway toward Mill Valley. I kept the back window cracked because I liked air blowing in my face. Car horns and the constant hum of tires against asphalt were all I heard, while trees and ocean views drifted past my field of vision. The idea of my brother being used as a weapon sent chills up and down my spine. I wouldn't relax until I'd heard from Agent Spencer that Austin was "clean."

Dad had to drive into town to drop off Dr. Loftus at his local office and by that time it was almost five o'clock. I didn't know about Austin, but I was starving.

"Can we pick up some pizza on the way home?" I asked as we pulled away from the waving Loftus.

Dad had stopped at a red light on Miller Avenue. "That's a

great idea. Okay with you, Leslie?" He glanced over at Mom as the light turned green.

"Sure. Sounds fine." Her voice sounded listless and far away.

"Call ahead and order, will you, Colton?" Dad headed the car down Miller in the direction of Extreme Pizza, our favorite family spot.

Agent Spencer had insisted we all leave our phones in the car when we went into the lab, maybe because she worried we'd snap pictures or record video. I slipped mine out of the pocket on the back of Mom's seat and speed-dialed Extreme Pizza. I ordered two larges—one pepperoni and one veggie. Mom always went for the veggie, Dad ate only pepperoni, and Austin and I ate both. At least he used to. We hadn't had pizza since his return.

Because everyone wanted pictures of The Ageless Kid, Austin and I stayed in the car with Mom, while Dad went in to pick up the pizzas. We waited about ten minutes, long enough for a fair number of people to walk by and stare. Our cars were well known in town.

I scooted down to avoid being seen and Austin copied me. I hated having to hunker down like soldiers in a foxhole, but what choice did we have with so many people trying to take our picture? We stayed like that until Dad opened the back door and slid two giant pizza boxes onto the seat next to me. The intoxicating smell of cheese and cooked veggies made my stomach rumble. I realized I hadn't even eaten a snack before we left the house for Homeland Security.

The moment we got home, Dad and I dug into the pizza like we hadn't eaten in a week. Mom just nibbled her slice and

Austin worked on the same piece for about ten minutes before leaving the crust on his plate. He'd never liked pizza crust, and I was happy to see that hadn't changed. It's funny, but little things like that eased my fear that Austin might not be the same anymore.

Later that night, Austin sat down to draw in his room. He'd grabbed some of my *Flash* comics and set them on his table, I guess because he liked the cover art and wanted to free-hand his own versions. His interest in *The Flash* was something else that hadn't changed from before, especially *Reverse Flash* (a villain from the future who replicated the Flash's powers and reversed his costume.)

Once he began drawing, I set my laptop onto his desk and popped it open to contact my crew. The Homeland Security thing happened so fast that I didn't have a chance to do anything but text everyone from the car what was going on.

They wanted all the details about the lab and the tests, especially Emily. She didn't mention our little "blowup" of the night before and neither did I. It was history.

"Hey, Fringe Girl, here," she said with a huge smirk. "Course I want to know about the top-secret stuff."

My friends' faces filled three corners of my screen, while mine occupied the fourth box. I glanced back at Austin, but he was busy drawing.

"I wish I could tell you, but I can't. My parents could go to prison for twenty years. That's no joke."

"Just a hint?"

I shook my head.

Keilani leaned in, looking worried. "Do you think what they tested Austin for might also apply to Kumaka?"

I paused because I hadn't thought of Kumaka. Could all these vanished kids have been kidnapped for the purpose of turning them into bombs? But why only the nonverbal ones? Then I almost slapped my forehead.

Idiot!

So, they couldn't tell where they'd been taken or what was done to them! It was a really scary notion, and I didn't want to go there.

"Not likely, Keilani," I answered, keeping my voice steady. "Even one of the agents said it was a long shot."

"Wish you could give us a hint," Casey put in, speaking clearly despite a mouthful of chicken, which he washed down with a swig of Coke. Maybe it was all that soccer practice, but Casey had an appetite that didn't quit. And he never got fat. Lean and mean, as the saying went.

Keilani looked downcast.

"What's up, Hawaiian Girl?" Emily asked. "Boyfriend troubles?" Even when she was trying to be sympathetic, her natural sarcasm leaked in.

Casey paused in the act of chewing.

Keilani shook her head. "I just wish I could meet Austin in person."

"Why?" That was Emily again. With her on chat, it was hard for the rest of us to say much. Talk about dominating the conversation. That was Em.

Keilani shrugged and brushed her long hair off her face. It was a little after five her time and she hadn't showered yet from surf practice. Her hair dangled around her shoulders like a dark mop.

"I feel like meeting him would connect me to Kumaka

somehow. I don't know why. It's dumb. But I just feel sure they went to the same place when they vanished."

I offered my best smile. "You're welcome to visit any time."

"Thanks, but we can't afford to fly to the mainland." She sounded dejected.

"You can afford to surf and that's an elitist sport," Emily put in, her tone more derisive than usual.

Keilani didn't look hurt because she knew Emily's acerbic style. "Hello, Fringe Girl, island over here? Not elitist when you're surrounded by water."

"She has a point," Casey piped up, always looking for a chance to score points with Keilani. "I'd love to learn."

Emily snorted, but Keilani smiled. "Come on over and I'll teach you, Cute Boy."

He grinned. "Hope I can one day. Soon."

"So, Colton, you ready for Anderson Cooper?" Keilani asked.

"Yeah, I think so."

"All the kids at school are planning to watch," Casey added, but he didn't look happy about it.

That caught my attention. "Good. I want 'em to."

"You do?"

"Yeah. Maybe they'll treat people better."

"What does that mean on my planet?" Emily asked.

"You'll see." Not even Casey knew what I was going to say. "You still down to watch Austin during the interview, Case?"

Casey nodded. "Yeah. My parents are excusing me from afternoon classes so I can come over. Be there at noon."

I smiled again. "Thanks, man." Then I yawned and my

entire body sort of caved in on itself. I'd been so stressed out all day worrying about Homeland Security, I was wiped.

"Gotta crash, guys. Another big day tomorrow."

"Can't wait to see you on TV," Keilani offered before she signed off. She sounded excited, but Emily kind of mad-dogged the camera. I wasn't sure what was up with that, but I decided I didn't want to know.

"Night, guys," I said, and ended the call.

I went to bed right after I helped Austin into his pajamas, but I slept poorly. I was probably restless thinking about those tests they did on my brother, but I was also nervous about my big interview the next day. I woke in the middle of the night and was startled to find Austin standing by the window staring out at the darkness beyond. Was this a nightly routine and I'd slept through it every time? I called to him, but he didn't even look at me. Could he have been doing this before, when he slept alone? Did aliens call to him from outside and he'd go to the window to "talk" with them? These thoughts danced around in my head until I grew sleepy and dropped off.

When I woke the next morning, Austin was at his drawing table creating a new piece of art. He seemed so focused that I didn't even glance over his shoulder to see what it was.

I realized much later that I should have.

When it was time for Dad to drive me to Dr. Bernstein, Austin wouldn't let us leave without him.

"It's my therapist, Austin," I explained, as though he could understand what I meant. "You can't go in with me."

He'd planted himself before the front door so Dad and I couldn't exit unless we went out the back. Mom stood off to the side and watched the scene unfold. Her hair was disheveled from cleaning, and I knew she'd been working all night to get the place spotless for the TV crew.

"Take him, Tom," she said, when Austin refused to move. "He can stay in the car with you."

So that's what we did.

Dr. Bernstein's craggy face broke into an enormous smile when I stepped into her *Star Wars* office twenty minutes later. I was so happy to see her, I impulsively gave her a hug. She hugged back, and for an old lady, she was hella strong.

I hadn't been to see her since Austin's return and her quiet office with its cool movie props and mellow lighting helped me unwind the moment I sat in that familiar recliner. I almost didn't want to talk or leave. I just wanted to luxuriate in this eye of the storm.

"You look well, Colton, happier than I've ever seen you."

I did? Since I never smiled much, how could she tell?

"I look different?"

She smiled warmly. "You *feel* different."

I nodded. I guess I did, at that. "Yeah. Having Austin home has been...." I wasn't sure, really. Had I even had time to think how it made me feel?

She waited and kept that open, inviting look on her face. One thing I loved about Dr. Bernstein is that she never put words into my mouth when I wasn't sure what to say. I wish all adults were like her.

"...confusing," I finally finished my thought. Because that's the best word I could come up with.

"That's a good word, Colton, given the circumstances of his return."

I nodded but wasn't quite sure where to go next.

"Tell me about this interview you have today," she said gently. "You mentioned on the phone that it was your idea."

"Yeah. I decided I'm going to confess everything."

Her eyebrows rose, but she didn't overreact. "I'm happy to hear that, Colton. But why on television instead of to your parents in private?"

I explained how I thought other kids might benefit from my story, and she listened with keen interest. I saw on her face that she was proud of my decision and that she respected it. That's what made her such an amazing therapist —she could communicate validation with just a look and a smile.

"If I may make an observation, Colton?"

"Course."

"When you entered my office five years ago, you were an angry, self-centered child."

My breath froze.

"But you have become one of the finest young men I have had the privilege of knowing," she went on, her voice tinged with admiration. "Your willingness to share your pain on national television so other kids won't have to go through the same self-hate and recrimination, well, that's above and beyond for most boys your age."

Michael J. Bowler

I felt so overwhelmed with swirling emotions that I just sat there like a stuffed animal with no voice box.

"In a way, Colton, Austin's disappearance, though it was a dark and traumatic event, helped you mold yourself into a decent human being. Had he never left the house that day, who knows where your anger would have led you."

I nearly gasped. I'd been so distraught over Austin's disappearance and my part in it, that I never realized how much it had changed me.

"You really believe that?"

"Yes. Sometimes, Colton, our darkest moments end up bringing us the most light."

Suddenly, the world seemed brand new, and I had hope that my life could go somewhere positive. Did it matter where Austin had been for the past five years? Of course, it did, and I wouldn't give up trying to figure out why he hadn't aged. But for me, for my life, it wasn't the most important thing. Having him home was what mattered most. I still worried about how my mother would react to my soon-to-be televised confession, so I shared with Dr. Bernstein what Dad had said about her "resenting" me (though it still felt like "hate" to me.)

"It's typical at your age to magnify emotional situations until they become greater than they perhaps are."

"I know," I said with an inward sigh. "I'm a hyperbolic teen, like Dad said. That what you mean?"

She offered a knowing smile. "You are dominated by the amygdala portion of your brain, Colton, as are all teenagers. That's the emotional engine, if you will, so yes, emotional situations tend to be larger than life. To a teen, something like resentment might easily translate as hate."

I considered her words. We'd learned about the brain in school, though I confess I hadn't paid much attention. "Do you think my mother will hate—" I stopped myself. "*Resent* me even more when she finds out?"

"I don't believe your mother ever hated you, Colton. I've told you that for five years. It is almost unheard of for a mother to hate her children. I doubt she even resents you. Not seriously, in any case. She's been hurt, just like you've been hurt. Your hurts have always expressed themselves as anger, which is not unusual in boys. Perhaps hers turn inward and manifest as the need to blame someone, though I can't say for certain since she isn't my patient."

Something about the way she said that about mothers not hating their children caused me to ask something I never had before. "Do you have kids, Dr. Bernstein?" She was so old, I guess I didn't think of her as parent material.

"Two. A boy and a girl. They're grown now."

This time *I* waited, like she'd modeled. I didn't want to put words in her mouth, but I sensed she wanted to say more.

"My son is an engineer with a wife and three beautiful children."

She smiled, and I did, too. It made me happy to hear that other people were happy.

"My daughter, on the other hand, hung around troubled kids in high school and got into drugs. She stole from me, was arrested on numerous occasions, has been in and out of rehab, and is still an addict. She blames me, Colton, because she said I paid more attention to my patients than I did to her. Perhaps I did. She says she hates me. But do I hate her? Never. And I always have hope for her."

135

I think my eyes bugged out as I listened. Her voice rippled with sadness, and I felt my chest tighten. But I understood her message loud and clear. "I'm sorry, Dr. Bernstein."

She offered her gentle smile again. "You know why I shared that story, Colton. I don't normally include patients in my personal life, but you need to understand how most mothers think or you'll never be fully at peace."

Her words echoed through my mind as I sat in the backseat beside Austin on the way home. Dad and I didn't talk. When I first started seeing Dr. Bernstein, Mom always wanted to know what we talked about and whether I found it helpful. I think I finally understood why she did that. But Dad didn't ask—he never did.

The house looked like the crowded halls of Tam High when the three of us entered through the open front door a short time later.

A large CNN van was parked in our driveway and several unfamiliar cars along with it. The paparazzi hovering on Marin View Avenue looked jealous as my dad drove past them and parked behind the van.

Men and women moved in and out the front door like ants, carrying lights, microphones, and cameras. They smiled at us as we entered and several paused to eye Austin with curiosity. I stayed close to him so the sudden flurry of activity wouldn't spook him in any way. He seemed oblivious, though, like he was taking his cues from me. I was nervous seeing all these people and equipment, but I kept it together for his sake.

The foyer was filled with light stands and two large cameras on rolling dollies. The activity was all between the foyer and the living room. I followed Dad, and Austin followed me.

As I stepped into the living room, Dad was extending his hand to Anderson Cooper, who had been chatting with Mom.

"Pleasure to meet you," Cooper said with quiet politeness. "Thank you for allowing us into your home, Mr. Bowman. I assure you we'll leave it exactly as we found it."

I glanced around and noticed that Dad's favorite chair and the large couch were angled in toward each other, I guess so we could all make eye contact during the interview. I figured Mr. Cooper would take the single chair, since he was the host.

I led Austin forward. Cooper was dressed in a dark suit with a purple tie and his silver hair almost shimmered beneath the bright television lights. He turned to me and grinned, as though we were best buds who hadn't seen each other in the longest.

"Hello, Colton." He extended a hand, and we shook.

"Hi, Mr. Cooper."

He pulled a mock frown. "Now, what did we agree to over the phone?"

It took me a second and then I remembered. "Oh, yeah. Hi, CNN Dude."

Mom gasped. "Colton!"

Cooper laughed and threw up his hand for a high five. I grinned and slapped it.

"No worries, Mrs. Bowman. Colton and I have an understanding."

He smiled and I felt at ease. All my tension melted away. He eyed Austin. Like everyone else, even this man who'd seen it all looked at my brother as though seeing a miracle.

"How's he doing?"

"He's the same, really," I answered. "It's like he never left."

Mom stepped forward now. I noticed she wore a dress, had

styled her hair off her face, and maybe even used her curling iron on it. I confess, I didn't study my mom's hair much, but it looked fancier than usual. And she wore earrings, too.

"Austin will be upstairs in his room with Colton's friend during the interview."

"I understand, Mrs. Bowman," Cooper replied, offering an understanding look. "I'm not here to exploit him or you. But your story is unique and important. I thank you again for the honor of interviewing you."

Mom blushed slightly. I guess she wasn't used to compliments from big-time celebrities.

Just then Casey entered the living room. "Hey, Colt, there you are. This place is lit up." He spotted Cooper and his mouth dropped open. "Whoa, it's CNN Dude!"

Mom gasped again, but Dad chuckled.

Cooper laughed. "I see Colton has been sharing my new name." He stuck out his hand. "CNN Dude at your service."

Casey shook his hand with vigor. "My mom is in love with you, sir. That's the truth."

Cooper smiled. "I'm guessing you're Casey."

"Yes, sir."

"Thank you for helping us out today."

"Hey, Colt is my best bud, you know?" He wore long pants, a polo shirt, and his soccer team jacket.

"I take it you play soccer, Casey."

"Yes, sir."

"He's really amazing, too," I added, feeling a desire to share Casey's accomplishments. "He's gonna go pro one day."

Cooper looked impressed. "Wow. I might be interviewing you at some point, huh?"

Casey grinned. It didn't take much to pump him up. "For sure."

"Colton, please take Casey and Austin upstairs and get them settled in," Mom said. I could tell she was worried that people coming and going might upset Austin.

I looked at Cooper. "What time will we start?"

He glanced at what looked like a very fancy wristwatch. "I'd say twenty minutes. Once you get them settled, come on down and I'll run through what we're going to do."

"You got it, CNN Dude." I ignored Mom's frown and led Austin from the room. Casey followed.

As soon as we entered his room, Austin made straight for the window and stared out at the woods beyond. I gazed at my brother for a long moment, wondering about nanites and alien abductions and whether I'd ever know if he forgave me.

"Uh, what should I do with him?"

I turned to Casey and shrugged. "He might stand there all afternoon. Or he might sit down to draw. Hard to say."

"'Kay. I have homework to knock out anyway." He slipped off his backpack and dropped it to the floor beside Austin's bed. "Can I sit at his desk?"

"He never uses it. Always sits on the floor to draw. That's why we got him that low table and put it in front of the closet door mirror."

"Cool."

I indicated the table, glancing at mine and Casey's reflection in the full-length mirror. For a moment, I flashed back to how we looked as young boys. We were both so tall now, me dark-haired and he blond, and yet our boyish faces looked the same. Just like Austin looked the same.

He peered at me a long moment.

"What?"

"You ready for this? The interview and all?"

I tensed up but nodded. I could do this. I had to. "It's time everyone heard my story."

He looked at me in a shy kind of way, not the boisterous manner he used at school. "Anything in there I don't know?"

"Yeah."

"Oh." He looked hurt.

"I just couldn't talk about it, Case, with anybody except Dr. Bernstein. But it's been eating me up, you know, and I need to get it out there."

He placed a hand on my shoulder. "Whatever it is, I got your back."

"Thanks." I glanced again at Austin, but he was oblivious. "I better get downstairs."

I left the room and closed the door.

Mr. Cooper was awesome about helping me relax during rehearsal. We sat on the sofa, and he took over Dad's big chair, as I'd suspected he would. He asked some general questions about the weather and how we liked living in Mill Valley, stuff like that. My guess is he was saving the real questions for the taping but wanted us to feel comfortable with him.

When he asked me how I liked school, I pulled a face. "I tolerate it, but I really hate some of the stupid classes they make us take."

"So did I," he agreed. "I think that's pretty universal."

He asked me to describe some of my art projects, and I did. He sounded really impressed when I told him about my paintings and the awards I'd won.

"I'd love to see your work sometime, Colton," he enthused. "Do you have any samples here?"

I pointed to a large painting on the wall to his left. It was an oil rendition of the woods of Mount Tam (big surprise, huh?) with almost 3D-looking rain in the foreground and a rainbow stretching off into the horizon in the background.

"Wow!"

His reaction was genuine, and I felt pride in myself. "That one got first place in the county last year."

He turned away from the painting and grinned. "I can see why. You must be very proud of him, Mr. and Mrs. Bowman."

I glanced down, afraid of what my parents might say. But Dad was right there with, "I couldn't be prouder," and my heart filled with warmth.

"He's going on to art school," Mom added, but I couldn't tell from her tone whether she approved. She still wanted me to be an architect like Dad.

"I'd love to buy one of your paintings, Colton," Cooper said, and I almost fell off the couch.

"Wow, thanks!" I gushed. "Some of my stuff is still at school, but I can send you pictures of all my work."

"I look forward to it."

A man with a clipboard stepped over and gave Cooper a thumbs up. While we'd been chatting, the two camera operators had been moving around, catching the best angles, and the lighting guys tinkered with the lights, so they lit our faces, but didn't blind us. We also had small microphones clipped to our collars and I guessed the sound guys had been testing levels too.

"We're ready to begin taping," Cooper said. "Don't worry if you make a mistake. We'll edit that out before it airs."

I nodded, and so did my parents.

The interview began with Cooper looking straight at one camera and introducing himself like he always does on TV. Then he turned to us and said, "Tonight, we welcome the Bowman family, who need little introduction. But for those viewers who might not have seen my coverage of this story five years ago, here's a brief recap. Their fifteen-year-old son, Austin, disappeared one afternoon. His parents hired private detectives, the FBI was involved, and police throughout the country ran his photo through their database. But not a trace of Austin was found. His younger brother, Colton, sitting with me tonight, spent the past five years devoting most of his free time to finding Austin. I want to begin with him. Colton, please tell us how it felt to lose your brother that way."

I momentarily froze, despite the camaraderie we built up during rehearsal. I guess I didn't expect that question. "It was the worst feeling ever. Like I was dying."

He asked my parents the same question and they described how devastated and afraid they'd been.

"Only a parent who's lost a child could understand how we felt," Mom added solemnly.

"That's completely understandable, Mrs. Bowman," Cooper agreed. He turned to the camera again. "As you all know, that wasn't the end of the story. Five years elapsed and then, Colton, could you tell us what happened last week?"

I described how weird I'd felt at school and how I'd needed to get home and then how Austin just appeared in the driveway. My hands were sweating, and I pressed my palms against my pants to keep them dry.

"And that's when you saw that Austin hadn't aged over the five years," Cooper put in when I paused.

"Yeah. It freaked me out. Freaked all of us out." I glanced at Dad and Mom because I figured they should tell this part.

Cooper asked them how they felt about Austin's present condition and Dad said, "Colton used the right term. Freaked out."

He described all the medical tests Austin had undergone and confirmed that every one of them came back normal. Needless to say, he didn't mention Homeland Security. We still hadn't heard from Agent Spencer, but I didn't want to think about that right then.

"Any theories of your own?" Cooper asked, his voice calm and steady.

Mom and Dad glanced at each other anxiously and then Mom turned to me and shook her head. I was momentarily taken aback. Dad and I had already talked about sharing our alien abduction suspicions and now Mom was telling me not to? Was that what she meant by shaking her head? I looked at Dad. He appeared kind of guilty and gave a slight shake of the head, too.

I felt like I'd been sandbagged. Here I was on the spot, cameras rolling, and they spring something new on me? My anger took over my brain and I turned back to Cooper. "I think he was taken by aliens."

Mom gave a tiny gasp, but I didn't turn to face her.

I expected Cooper to react in some way, but he just looked casual. "I've heard that theory bandied about. What makes you believe it?"

I plowed forward and told him about Keilani and Kumaka

and the rain and the other kids we'd found who disappeared in the same fashion, and he listened intently to every word.

"Now that he's back and hasn't changed at all and he's healthy, what else could have kept him young but alien technology?" I watched his reaction to my question, and I could see that he was wondering the same thing. I still refused to look at my parents. I figured Mom was mad, but that was her fault. If she didn't want me to talk about this, she should've told me ahead of time.

"I confess, Colton, I'm no expert on so-called alien phenomena," Cooper said with careful deliberation, "But I can't think of a case with more convincing evidence than Austin's. There is, as yet, no earthly explanation."

"We're continuing the search for answers, Mr. Cooper," Dad offered as he shifted slightly beside me. I heard in his voice the underlying fear of what Agent Spencer might still tell us. "Leslie and I are not of the opinion that aliens were involved because there is no physical evidence to back up that theory."

"Dad!" I hissed, turning to face him. He refused to meet my eye.

"None of the medical tests revealed anything extraterrestrial," Dad went on, his arm around Mom. She refused to meet my eye, too. "I know Colton still thinks it's possible, but we'll continue to pursue earthly explanations for Austin's unchanged condition."

Cooper faced me again. I guess he saw the anger, or maybe it was betrayal, on my face because he asked, "What do you want to say, Colton?"

I wanted to say, "Thanks for nothing, Dad!" but I guess I'd grown up enough over the past five years to have some self-control because I held my tongue. I was still mad, though, and thought of what Dr. Bernstein had said about Mom and her fears. Dad was protecting her, I guess, to keep her from more pain. And imagining space aliens out there just waiting for their chance to swoop in and steal Austin away again was too much hurt to bear.

I said, "Most abductees aren't taken just once, Mr. Cooper. My parents might not believe, but I do and that's why I'm sleeping in Austin's room every night now. No one will ever take him again without a fight."

My voice had risen slightly, and I realized I'd balled my hands into fists.

Cooper studied me a moment and asked the question I most needed: "I know he's your brother, Colton, but your obsessive devotion to finding him, and now with your desperate desire to protect him—you've gone above and beyond for a sibling. Is there an underlying reason?"

This was the moment of truth. I forced myself to keep eye contact with him. "It was my fault he ran away." My voice came out low, almost like a whisper. I heard Mom gasp, but I kept my eyes on Cooper's calm face.

"What do you mean?"

I swallowed hard and haltingly explained what happened that day with Casey, without mentioning what he said. I knew Casey's mom would watch the interview when it aired, and I wasn't a snitch.

"I'd lost so many friends because of Austin, because he was weird and different and, I don't know, I just snapped. I barged into his room and got in his face. I told him I...." I had to catch my breath. "I told him I hated him and that he was ruining my life and that I wished...he was dead. Then I told him to disappear. And he did, right after I said that!"

My voice trembled and I was on the verge of tears. Mom gasped again and even Dad made a kind of breathy sound. But I couldn't look. No way. Would I see anger on Dad's face? Hate on Mom's?

Cooper looked touched. "Kids say things like that all the time, Colton. You were only twelve. I'm sure you didn't mean it."

"I didn't, I swear I didn't!" My voice sounded raspy, even to me, and I wished for some water. "But Austin didn't know that. And that's why he ran. And then he disappeared and I..."

"You felt responsible?"

I nodded. "And I was so afraid my parents would hate me for what I did that I never told anyone except my therapist."

Mom made another audible sound, but I didn't turn my head.

"I never even told Casey."

"Why are you telling us now, Colton, on national television?"

I paused to collect my thoughts because I didn't want this to come out wrong. "Partly because I don't have to be looking at my parents, in case, you know, they hate me for it."

"Colton." That was Dad. I felt him move beside me.

"I need to finish, Dad," I said firmly, without breaking eye contact with Cooper. "Please."

Dad settled back in the couch, and I said, "But mostly it's 'cause of what I hear at school. I hear kids on their phones cussing out their moms or siblings or friends and saying really nasty things. Or they brag about texting really nasty things, like what I said to Austin. And I bet a lot of teenagers like me have lost people they said something bad to. I just want kids to understand that we never know what might happen and that we should never, you know, talk mess to people we love and leave it at that. I went to Austin's room after I thought over what I'd said. I wanted to apologize. But I never got the chance."

Cooper looked impressed. "That's very considerate of you, Colton, to think of the greater good within your own pain and guilt. Now that Austin is back, have you apologized?"

I nodded. "'Cept, I don't know if he understands or if he forgives me. I just wish I knew—"

"Austin!"

That was Mom.

I swiveled my head around and sucked in a breath. Austin stood at the entrance to the living room.

Footsteps pounded down the stairs and a breathless Casey lurched to a stop beside him. "I'm so sorry, Mr. and Mrs. Bowman. He just got up and left the room and I was afraid to touch him and...."

"It's okay, Casey," Dad said.

I forgot all about Cooper and the interview and focused on my brother. He held a piece of paper in one hand. A drawing. I could see that much.

"Colton, take your brother back to his room." Mom was fighting to keep her voice steady. The cameras were still rolling, but none of us thought about that until later.

Austin didn't wait for me to rise. He strode across the room while Casey looked on helplessly from the doorway. Austin stopped right in front of me and fixed those unfathomable eyes on mine.

147

"Austin? You okay?"

He didn't respond.

"Austin, I'm Mr. Cooper," I heard from my left, but couldn't take my eyes off my brother.

"Colton, please." That was Mom again.

Austin handed me the drawing.

I glanced down, and nearly choked.

In Austin's almost photographic portrayal, my angry face leapt off the page, ripped through my heart, and stabbed at my soul. My fists were balled up and my eyes filled with hate, my face very close to Austin's. We were in front of his window, and he had his left arm extended, pointing to something outside.

What tore me apart was the realization that I was wearing the same tank top, the one from that terrible day five years before. And I looked younger. I looked twelve. And Austin stood taller than me.

He had recreated the worst moment in both our lives with such stunning clarity that I felt like I was back there, in that room, at that time, shouting those hateful words at him.

I knew what this drawing meant. He didn't forgive me. My eyes welled up and I couldn't stop the tears.

"Austin, please forgive me. I didn't mean it, not a word!" He just stared. "I swear to you I would take back every word if I could. I beg you, Austin, forgive me. Please!"

Tears rolled down my cheeks, but Austin remained impassive. He turned and strode past Casey and back upstairs. His footfalls echoed slightly because of the dead silence in the room.

"Colton, what's that drawing?" Dad asked quietly.

"Please show us," Mom added, her voice filled with worry. "What's going on?"

"Colton, stay with me here." That was Cooper.

But my gaze remained riveted to the doorway through which Austin had disappeared. I vaguely caught Casey's look of helpless shock and heard my parents and Cooper trying to get my attention. But I tuned them out. As more tears erupted, I leaped up from the couch and tossed the drawing onto the floor before bolting from the room. I swept past Casey.

"Colt!"

I ignored Casey and took the stairs two at a time before slamming my door and throwing myself face down onto the bed. I soaked my pillow with tears.

Chapter 11

Agent Spencer Called

I had no idea how much time passed before I heard a knock on my door.

"Colt, it's me."

"Go away, Case," I said—partly into my pillow, so it came out garbled. "I don't want you to see me crying."

"Bro, I've seen you cry before." Even through the wood of the door, he sounded worried.

"Okay, come in."

The door opened and Casey stepped inside.

I rolled over onto my back and wiped tears away with my sleeve. I almost never wore long sleeve shirts and only did today for the interview. But the sleeve came in handy with my wet face.

"I ruined everything, didn't I?"

He sat on my bed and looked at me with the same compassion he had five years before when he'd apologized.

"No way, dude. What you said rocked. I never knew what

happened after I left that day." He looked kind of shy again, which he usually did when emotions other than humor were involved. "Wish you told me, instead of keeping it inside."

"I couldn't. Not saying it almost made me feel like it never happened."

"Your mom was gonna go after you, but your dad told her to stay and finish the interview. Since I was already on camera. Mr. Cooper asked me to take your place."

I raised my eyebrows and sat up against the headboard. "Yeah? What'd you say?"

His face shifted slightly, and he glanced down at my bedcovering. "I knew my mom would be watching later, so I confessed that it was my fault you got mad at Austin. I told them what I said and how bad I felt after he disappeared. And that I'd never come clean about it, to my mom or the kids at school, because I was too embarrassed. I pretended you went psycho on me for no reason, remember?"

"What made you tell the truth now?"

He looked up and offered a little grin. "My best friend confessed, so I figured I should, too."

Despite my pain at Austin's lack of forgiveness, I returned the grin, and we bumped fists. I'll be forever grateful for Casey's friendship. And I realized something significant in that moment. Friends will never be perfect. They will let you down. But the true ones always own up and make things right.

There was another knock and I looked up to see Dad standing in the doorway.

"Interview over?" I asked.

He nodded.

"I'm sorry, Dad, for running off and messing it up. But that drawing...." My breath hitched and I couldn't go on.

He looked guilty, which surprised me. "Colton, you should have told us before."

"So, Mom could hate me even more?"

"Your mother never hated you, son. I told you that. She just was upset and distraught and wasn't thinking when she blamed you."

"Then why isn't she here telling me that?"

Dad fidgeted. "The interview and Austin's picture gave her a stress headache. She went to lie down."

That meant she didn't want to face me. Mom was pretty easy to read. Guess Dr. Bernstein was wrong, after all.

"Uh, Anderson is leaving and wants to say good-bye."

I pulled my legs up and Casey stood so I could swing them over the side of the bed. "I'll come right down."

"No need. He's here."

Dad stepped aside and Mr. Cooper entered my room. He offered that little smile he had, as though seeing me made his whole day. His gaze shifted to the artwork on my walls. Some were forest scenes, like the one downstairs. But others were portraits of famous people like Martin Luther King and Leonardo da Vinci. I'd learned different formats, so some were oils, others watercolor or pastel. I'd even done some in manga-style—characters from anime, like Deku from a show called *My Hero Academia*.

A few paintings depicted the insides of alien spaceships. Others portrayed rain and rainbows. My favorite was a charcoal of Austin. It was a three-quarter view of him staring intently out his bedroom window at the forest beyond, and somehow the plain charcoal and absence of color made his face look more haunting than ever.

Cooper nodded approvingly. "You and I will definitely be doing business, Colton."

I grinned and wiped the remaining tears off my cheeks.

"Your dad said if you agree, we'll air the entire interview, including your reaction to Austin's drawing."

I scrunched up my face in confusion. "Why would you do that? It'll look lame and ruin the whole show."

"On the contrary, Colton, it will galvanize the viewers."

"Huh?"

"You said on air that you want kids to know the pain of saying hateful things and not getting closure with the people they hurt. Your emotional reaction to Austin's drawing sent that message more strongly than a thousand words ever could. But I don't want to embarrass you, Colton. If you say no, I'll have it deleted."

I glanced at Dad.

"This is your call, son."

I turned to Casey standing beside the bed. "What do you think, Case? Kids at school gonna start in on me again?"

"If they do, I'll shut 'em down like before. They don't matter anyway, Colt."

I considered his words. Those kids *did* matter. That's why I'd confessed on air. I faced Cooper. "Run it."

He smiled. "You're an impressive young man, Colton. Do you have a phone?"

Confused, I reached into my pocket and slipped it out.

"May I see it?"

I unlocked the screen and handed it over. He pushed some buttons and then typed something.

"What are you typing?"

"My personal cell number. You and I have business to conduct, remember?"

I nodded, stunned that a big-time celebrity would give me his private number.

"And I hope you'll just call me sometimes, to let me know how you're doing. Will you do that?"

I was stunned that this total stranger liked me enough to want to keep in touch.

"I'd like that."

He turned the phone around to show me what he'd typed. There was a number and the name "CNN Dude."

I grinned as I took back the phone. "Thanks, CNN Dude."

He chuckled and Dad escorted him out.

Afraid of facing Mom, I asked Casey to hang around for dinner, but he said he had to go home.

"I need to be with my parents when the interview airs."

I understood. "Chat afterwards?"

"Yeah. We'll get the girls on and see what they thought. Who knows, Colt, you and me might be headed for the big time. You know, reality TV."

He laughed, we bumped fists, and he took off.

I couldn't face Austin, so I stayed in my room until dinner. I guess Mom didn't want to see me because she didn't even come downstairs. Austin did, though, on his own, and acted like he hadn't ripped my heart out and stomped it into mush with that drawing. Dad tried to serve him some leftover casserole, but he refused to cooperate until I gave him his food. Only then did he eat.

I tried to avoid looking up when I felt his eyes on me, even though his eyes never revealed any emotion. After dinner, Dad asked me to take Austin to his room, but he stood up and left the kitchen on his own. I guess he didn't want to be around me anymore, and that made me feel more empty than ever.

I stayed in my room until Dad called me down to watch the interview on CNN. I didn't want to because Mom would be there, but Dad insisted.

"You need to see the whole thing, Colton."

We had a seventy-inch flat screen in the family room and a sofa where we usually all sat to watch movies. But this time, I sat across the room in a separate chair.

Mom looked drawn and worried when she entered, almost guilty.

"You okay, Mom?"

"Yes, Colton. Thanks for asking. My headache is better."

That was all she said.

She sat next to Dad on the sofa and Anderson Cooper's show began.

They did a really good job of editing, I guess, because I didn't look nearly as scared as I'd felt. The interview went great, even though it was obvious I got mad when Dad shot down the alien abduction theory. The camera cut to Austin in the doorway. My body tensed up and I think I held my breath during most of that part until my onscreen self bolted from the room. Then Cooper called Casey over and I relaxed a bit, since I was no longer on camera.

Casey confessed that he had started the fight that day. "I

called Austin a retard," he explained, his voice rife with shame, "and that's why Colt punched me. I deserved it, too."

Mom on TV looked guilty, and I was afraid to look at her seated across from me now.

Cooper turned to her and asked, "Mrs. Bowman, how do you feel about what Casey said? And what Colton said earlier, when he expressed fear that you'd hate him for what he did?"

Mom looked like she might cry any moment. "Thank you, Casey, for telling the truth." Her voice sounded tight, like a guitar string that might snap any second. "It's true I blamed Colton for Austin running away, but I never knew what happened between them. I was distraught and terrified. I slapped my son, Mr. Cooper."

The camera cut to Cooper, but he kept his cool like always.

In the interview, Dad reached out to take Mom's hand, and though I wasn't watching them at that moment, I felt sure he was doing the same thing right now.

On screen, Mom cleared her throat. "I said terrible things to my son and treated him horribly for a long time, but I never hated Colton. Not for one minute. He was a difficult child, what with the fights at school and his negative attitude toward his brother, but I never stopped loving him. He's my son. I couldn't hate him if I tried."

My mouth went dry, and my eyes welled with tears. This time I did look over at Mom and found her gazing at me. Her expression wasn't angry or even guilty. She looked fearful, like I might not forgive her.

"Colton has become an incredible young man," Mom on screen was saying. "In spite of my demeaning him, he's blossomed, and I wish I could take back every negative word and every angry glare I ever gave him."

I turned back to the TV as Mom looked right into the camera. "I'm sorry, Colton. I hope you can forgive me." A tear trickled from her eye and Dad pulled her in close.

I looked across the room at Mom—she was crying. I was too. I leaped up and passed in front of the TV. She stood awkwardly and I threw my arms around her. We held each other close and cried. I was vaguely aware of the interview continuing, of Dad saying that he hoped "my family can be a family again, even if we never learn the truth about Austin."

Dad stood and wrapped both arms around Mom and me while Cooper, on television, wrapped up the interview in the background.

This had been a day for confessions and making things right. And like Dr. Bernstein had been telling me for five years, there's no misunderstanding between friends or loved ones that can't be fixed. She was right.

I got a text from her shortly after the interview ended, short and sweet: *I've never been more proud of you.*

That choked me up big time. I typed: *Thanks. Couldn't have done it without you.*

She texted back a smile emoji.

I stayed in my room after that and contacted the crew. I wasn't sure Austin even wanted me to sleep in his room anymore.

The four boxes appeared on my screen, with Keilani and Emily occupying the two top and Casey and me the two bottom.

Keilani almost screamed when she saw me. "Oh, my God, Colton, that interview! I cried all through it."

Emily snorted with derision. "You did?"

Keilani nodded, and I noticed that her eyes looked puffy. She really *had* been crying.

"Why? Because I made a fool of myself?"

Her face crumpled with shock. "Colton, you have no idea how that interview made me feel. I don't think you can because it's hard to see yourself like other people do. But it was the most real moment I've ever seen on TV. It tore my heart apart."

Casey leaned closer, his face deadly serious for a change. "She's right, Colt. On TV, it was...different. I mean, I saw it happen live, but even I got all emotional watching it."

"Yeah?" That stunned me.

"Yeah."

I felt kind of shy and embarrassed with the girls there, but said, "Thanks for telling the truth like you did. That was straight up."

"Should 'a done it years ago." Casey looked guilty again.

"Enough of this emotionalism," Emily said with the usual snark in her voice. "The saccharine count is killing me here."

"Did you watch the interview, Emily?" I asked, not sure I wanted an answer.

"Course I did."

"And you're telling us you didn't find it touching?" Keilani sounded incredulous. "When Colton saw that drawing, his face looked so devastated and his voice so full of anguish, even my mom cried."

Emily glowered. "Course, I felt something, Hawaiian Girl. I just don't get all dewy-eyed over boys crying on camera." She paused, maybe because I looked mortified. "But I did find it illuminating and a bit...poignant."

Keilani shook her head in disgust. "Best review you'll get out of her, Colton, so you better take it."

"Course he will," Emily retorted. "Psycho Boy and me don't get all caught up in drama."

"Okay." That was all I said. What else was there? Emily wasn't much for emoting, but I'd learned not to judge kids the way I'd been judged. I'm sure her abduction experiences were way more terrifying than she ever let on.

Casey asked, "When you coming back to school, Colt?"

I frowned. The thought of going back didn't thrill me. "I think on Monday. My parents said it's my senior year and I need to finish it at school."

He grinned. "Awesome. I feel alone without you there."

"You have tons of friends," Emily tossed out with a roll of her eyes, "and, like, every girl at that school throwing herself at you."

Keilani frowned but said nothing.

"I do not," Casey insisted. He looked very serious, as though not sure what to say, which wasn't like him at all. "Okay, I am kind of popular because of the soccer and all."

"And the fact that you're cute," Emily put in with a smirk.

Keilani glowered, and that got me thinking.

Casey glanced up at Keilani's box, looking embarrassed. "Most of the kids are pretty superficial."

"Duh, Cute Boy," Emily added. "Could have told you that."

Casey looked exasperated. "Will you let me finish, Fringe Girl?"

She looked kind of stunned, like no one had ever told her to stop talking before.

Casey paused a moment, and then glanced in my direction. "You're the only real friend I have at that school, Colt. That's truth. The rest are just, I don't know the word, people I hang out with. That's why I felt so bad for lying." He paused a moment. "You know what?"

I shook my head.

"I hope people dump on me for telling lies about you. I deserve that."

My mouth dropped open.

"Drama Boy, here."

"Zip it, Fringe Girl!" snapped Keilani.

We all looked shocked by her reaction.

"I know you've been through it, too, Emily, with your abductions and all," Keilani went on. "But Colton and me have it way worse losing our brothers like we did. If you don't think so, well, then those aliens brought you back without a heart."

Emily was silent and stared at the screen in surprise.

"Casey," Keilani continued, not waiting for Emily to get started again. "I hope the kids don't dump on you, but what you did tonight, telling the truth like you did, it was amazing and I'm really happy you're my friend."

Casey looked awkward, almost an unheard-of reaction. "Uh, thanks, Keilani."

I knew I had to say something, because I'd always thought Casey was super happy being the center of attention. "I never knew that, Case, about me being you're only real friend at Tam. Thanks. You don't know how much I needed to hear that."

Casey offered his best smile. "I think I do."

I felt loved in a way I never had with my parents. It feels different when people outside your family let you know how much they value you. And not just Casey, either. Keilani's validation, and—in her own detached sort of way—Emily's. They all had my back and made me feel like I mattered.

We chatted a bit more, but then I signed off because, well, I was beat. All the emotions I'd been through that day had drained me. I guessed that was why Emily avoided them so staunchly.

I slipped on workout shorts and a t-shirt and went to my parents' room. In pajamas and robes, they sat up on their queen-sized bed talking in low tones.

"Uh, I just wanted to say good night."

Mom's lined face looked creased with worry, so I stepped closer to the bed.

Dad said, "I'm sorry, Colton, for backstabbing you on camera the way I did."

"That was my fault," Mom admitted. "I didn't want to validate the alien possibility."

I was confused. "Why not?"

"Partly because I can't face the idea that this might not be over, that Austin might be taken away from us again," Mom admitted, her voice trembling. "But I also thought about what Alysse and Emily have been through. I don't want you and your brother to be a freak show for the rest of your lives. I'm sorry I didn't warn you, but I literally made the decision during the taping."

I was shocked into silence. Whether or not aliens were truly involved, if my parents admitted on national television that abduction was the most likely explanation, we'd never hear the end of it. Tabloids would follow us around for years, like they've done to Alysse and Emily. Mom hadn't stabbed me in the back —she'd done me a favor.

"Thanks, Mom," I whispered.

She looked surprised but said nothing. I could tell something more was on her mind.

"What's wrong?"

Dad looked almost afraid. "With all the excitement today, Colt, we just realized that Agent Spencer never called."

I froze. I'd forgotten, too! "What do you think that means?"

"I've been telling your mother that the tests might have taken longer to read. I'm certain if Agent Spencer thought there was any danger, she'd have called right away."

I sagged with relief. That sounded reasonable.

"We also couldn't get Austin to change for bed," Mom put in, her voice filled with sadness. "I don't know why he won't let me do things for him anymore. But I don't resent you because he wants your help."

I guess Dad told her about our conversation.

"Thanks."

I had figured since Austin didn't forgive me that he'd go back to letting Mom help him. I guess that wasn't so. I stood there, uncertain of my role anymore. Austin had wanted me close since his return, but that drawing proved he was still mad, so I didn't know what to do.

Dad seemed to read my thoughts, as he so often had these past few years. "The drawing doesn't necessarily mean he hates you, Colt. It might just be such a powerful memory that he wanted you to know he never forgot. We really can't know what he's thinking."

I considered that. And could I change how he felt? I'd apologized over and over. What else could I do? I was thinking that he didn't want me in his room anymore, but maybe that was wrong, too.

"Want me to see if he'll go to bed when I'm there?"

Mom nodded. "I know it's been a tough day for you, Colton. For all of us. But I think he still needs you."

"Okay."

I found Austin sitting at his table working on a new drawing. I wasn't sure I wanted to see, but I stepped closer and looked over his shoulder. It was a clearing in the woods. I saw colored light, but no rainbow. Not exactly. More like shimmers of color all around. And there were people in the clearing. I leaned in because the people were so small compared to the towering trees. I gasped when I realized that the people were us, our family. The hand-drawn Austin looked exactly like the real deal, but I had... blond hair? And Mom had red! Huh? Dad looked pretty much the same, and so did Mom and me, I guess, except for the hair, but why would Austin draw us that way? In truth, his picture kind of creeped me out.

I fought back a yawn. "Uh, Austin, it's time for bed. Want me to help you get your pajamas on?"

He put down the colored pencil and stood to face me. Hesitant, I moved closer and took the hem of his shirt in my fingers. He made no move to resist. I pulled it up and he lifted his arms so the shirt came off. I held the waistband of his pants while he stepped out of them. Then I grabbed some pajamas from his dresser drawer, and he put them on.

He strode to his bed, but didn't get in. He stood beside my sleeping bag and waited.

Feeling a rush of conflicting emotions, I stepped forward and looked Austin in the eye. "You're sure, Austin? You still want me here?"

He placed one foot on the sleeping bag. My mouth dropped open and my heart pounded. He might not have forgiven me, but he hadn't rejected me.

I turned off the light and dropped to the floor. As I slid into the bag, he clambered into his bed and pulled the covers to his chin. I lay there in the dark listening to my brother breathe, and I felt hopeful.

When I brought Austin down for breakfast the next morning, I found Mom cleaning and scrubbing the kitchen raw. The tiles were gleaming. That meant she was worried or upset, especially since she'd already scoured everything the day before.

"Mom? What's wrong?"

She turned in startled shock, and then deflated before my eyes. "Colton. You scared me. Nothing's wrong."

I stared at her, Austin at my side. I knew she was lying.

"Agent Spencer called."

I froze. "And?"

"They're coming over this morning to talk to us."

I fought to keep my voice steady. "Did she say anything about the test results?"

"She said I shouldn't worry, but I guess I can't help but worry. Why come over here if everything was normal?"

Good question, I thought. But I didn't say it.

"I'm sure it's nothing big or she'd have said something." Would she? Over an unsecured phone line? My fringy side was screaming.

She tossed off a grateful smile. "You boys sit. I'll whip up some scrambled eggs."

"Thanks, Mom."

Dad came down a short while later and we had a nice family breakfast of eggs and toast and some skillet potatoes. Dad and Mom put on a good show, but I knew they were nervous about what the agents might say.

I decided to ask something that Casey and I had talked about. "Could we go on a vacation this summer? The whole family?"

Dad's eyebrows rose and Mom looked surprised. We hadn't been on a family vacation since before Austin vanished.

"That's a great idea, son," Dad said with real enthusiasm. Even Mom cracked a smile. "Anywhere in particular?"

Here goes nothing. "How about Maui?" I plowed ahead before they could protest. "I'd love to meet Keilani and her mom in person and it's really peaceful there and...well, Keilani wants to meet Austin. She thinks it will make her feel that Kumaka is still alive somewhere."

Mom's smile kind of froze on her face and then morphed into a look of sadness. "That poor girl. I've been so consumed with having Austin home, I didn't even think of her pain. What do you think, Tom? I'd love to meet Mele in person."

That was Keilani's mom. The two ladies had struck up a

Discord friendship of their own over the years, like Keilani and me.

"Works for me," Dad replied around a mouthful of eggs. He eyed me as he chewed. "You and Keilani an internet item?"

I almost blushed. Dad and I had talked about girls over the years, and I suspect he thought I should have a girlfriend by now. Keilani was amazing, but I knew how Casey felt about her, and she seemed more like my sister, anyway, because we'd both lost a brother.

I shook my head. "But Casey's got it bad for her. If we go over this summer, him and his parents will go, too. He's dying to hang out with her."

Dad swigged some orange juice. "I'll talk to Ralph and we'll make the arrangements. It'll be fun."

I finished my breakfast in silence. Keilani would probably scream when I told her the news. Just the thought of her reaction made me feel good for having thought of it. Now I just had to worry about what Homeland Security was going to tell us.

Chapter 12

What Do You Think It Means?

Agents Spencer and Martin arrived at ten. She was dressed in a navy-blue pantsuit and he in a gray suit with a somewhat flashy yellow tie. I guess because most of the media had left after CNN got our exclusive, the agents didn't have to pretend to be door-to-door salespeople anymore.

Dad ushered them into the living room, which, true to Mr. Cooper's word, had been put back exactly as they'd found it. Mom sat stiffly in one chair, Dad lowered himself into his stuffed armchair, and I sat in the loveseat, leaving the agents the big couch.

Austin stayed upstairs drawing more pictures of the woods with the little people wandering around, which still unnerved me.

"So," Dad began, his tone as even as he could keep it, "what did you find?"

Dad always got straight to the point. I liked that.

"Nothing," Agent Spencer replied.

Mom made a small sound and almost collapsed in on herself.

"I told you that on the phone, Mrs. Bowman," Spencer went on, offering Mom a smile of encouragement. "As far as our equipment and our scientists are concerned, Austin is clean. No sign of, well, what we *didn't* talk about the other day." She winked at me.

Dad wasn't quite satisfied. "As far as your equipment is concerned? What does that mean?"

Martin spoke, crisp and clipped. "The technology is too new and cannot be considered one hundred percent effective, Mr. Bowman. There is a three percent margin of error, which means we are ninety-seven percent certain Austin is clean."

Mom and Dad exchanged a look of worry.

"Ninety-seven percent is pretty high," I offered, hoping to ease their fears.

Dad glanced my way. "You're right, Colton." He turned back to the agents. "Thank you for your efforts."

Mom gazed at them with a worried intensity. "You could have told us that over the phone. Is there another reason you drove all the way out here?"

Spencer smiled and turned to Martin.

He looked slightly uncomfortable. "I wished to speak with Colton."

"Me?" I sat up straighter and stared across the room at him. "Why?"

"I watched your interview last night and I was most impressed."

Mom and Dad looked as mystified as I felt.

"Uh, thanks."

Martin looked at me with an intense gaze that reminded me of Austin. "And I'd very much like to see that drawing your brother created."

"What for?"

"Because I feel you may be misinterpreting its meaning."

My heart pounded and my mind whirled with questions.

"You should let him see it, Colton," Spencer said quietly. "His deductive skills are impeccable. But it's up to you."

"It can't hurt, Colton," Mom offered.

"I agree," Dad added.

"'Kay. Be right back."

I took the stairs two at a time and entered my room. I'd buried the picture at the bottom of my underwear drawer because I felt like crap every time I saw it. I purposely didn't look at my angry face as I slid it out and pelted back down the stairs. Slightly out of breath, I crossed the living room and handed the drawing to Agent Martin. He studied it carefully, his eyes squinting with concentration. Spencer peered over his shoulder. I bounced nervously on my heels.

After a few long moments, Martin looked up from the paper. Like Austin, his facial expression hardly ever changed. But his light brown eyes were lively and conveyed most of his emotions, near as I could tell. At the moment, I saw understanding.

"You are proceeding on the assumption that Austin doesn't forgive you because he gave you an angry demeanor in this drawing. Is that correct?"

I nodded stiffly.

"Does this image accurately represent what happened that afternoon just before he left the house?"

I nodded again.

"I call your attention, Colton, to this right here."

He pointed to something on the drawing, and I stepped around to examine it. His finger touched Austin's arm, the one that pointed out at the rainy woods. "Perhaps this is what he wants you to see and remember."

"He was pointing at the woods or maybe the rainbow. He did that more than once. He was nutty for rainbows." I didn't understand where Martin was going with this.

"Perhaps he was telling you that he planned to run away and now he's reminding you that it was his choice, not your words, that precipitated that action."

I gasped, then studied the image again. Is that what Austin had been trying to tell me? That he wanted to go, or maybe *had* to go? Like maybe someone was calling him? I remembered him at Dr. Loftus's window. I thought he'd stooped low to see something, but what if he'd been listening? I pictured that moment, how he looked, and recalled that his ear was tilted toward the colored bands of light. In fact, those colors had splashed across the left side of his face, and it sure looked like he was listening for something. Or someone.

"That's super possible," I muttered, my head spinning. "Could he have heard something out there that drew him into the woods?"

Martin raised his eyebrows. "What makes you say that?"

I recounted Austin's odd behavior in Loftus's office and both agents listened with avid interest.

"And you heard nothing when you stood next to him?"

Martin asked, his head tilted slightly as he considered the possibilities of what I'd told him.

I shook my head.

He went on in his flat tone of voice, "It's entirely possible Austin can hear at wavelengths you and I cannot."

"What does that mean, Agent Martin?" That was Dad, sounding worried again.

The agent turned his deadpan face toward Dad. "Unknown. But it bears further study." He turned back to me. "I suggest you observe him closely, Colton. If you note other behaviors of that sort, you may feel free to call me."

"We'd be happy to offer whatever assistance we can," Spencer added. Her tone of voice was understanding, and I could tell she really did want to help. I guessed government people weren't all bad, despite what Emily said.

Martin handed me back the drawing. "Thank you for showing me and for sharing your insights. I find this case most intriguing, however Agent Spencer and I have other duties to perform at this time."

He stood and Spencer stood beside him.

"That's my partner," she said with a chuckle. "Always onto the next job."

Mom and Dad stood and shook hands with both agents.

"Thank you," Dad gushed. "You had us worried for a while."

"Sorry, sir," Martin said. "Just doing our job."

Mom gave Spencer a hug. "I really appreciate you coming out here to help Colton the way you did." She turned to Martin. "May I hug you, Agent Martin?"

He looked uncertain. "Hugs are not part of our job description."

Spencer elbowed him good-naturedly. "They aren't forbidden, either."

Martin eyed her a moment and then turned to Mom. "Very well."

She reached out and hugged him. He stood stiffly as she did, while Spencer stifled a grin behind her hand.

As she stepped back, Martin extended his hand to me. I shook it.

"As a child growing up on the spectrum, Colton Bowman, I would have been exceedingly grateful to have had a brother like you."

I almost gagged. He released my hand and gazed at me with what looked like admiration.

"Thanks, Agent Martin." Then I burned red with embarrassment. "I'm really sorry for thinking you were weird."

He offered what could have passed for a smile. "I am weird. And apology accepted."

I grinned as he turned and strode toward the foyer. "Coming, Agent Spencer?"

"Be right there, partner."

Martin vanished from my view. I heard the front door open and close.

Spencer turned to us. "So, what's next?"

"We might be back to the alien abduction theory," I said, thinking that's what she meant, "now that it's possible someone or something might have called to him from the woods." I glanced at Mom and Dad. "But we'll keep it on the down low, so the media stays away."

She nodded approvingly to me but turned to my parents. "I meant for your family."

"We're going to take a vacation," Dad replied, "and live our lives."

"We'll keep trying to find out what happened to Austin," Mom added, slipping her arm through Dad's. "But I'm happy he's home and that we're whole again. Life goes on."

Spencer smiled. "Indeed, it does. Best success to you all." She turned to me. "You most of all, Colton. You'd make quite a detective yourself one day. Think about it."

And then she strode into the foyer and let herself out the front door.

I gazed at Mom and Dad for a long moment. "We should invite Alysse and Emily over like we talked about before. Especially now. Just to be sure."

Mom nodded. "Tomorrow's Saturday. I'll invite them for lunch."

"Cool." I still held the drawing in my hand and stole another look at it. But this time my eyes went to Austin's pointing finger, rather than my angry face.

What are you trying to tell me, Austin?

I texted Casey that my parents were up for the Maui trip, and he was super stoked.

Let's tell Keilani tomorrow after lunch, he texted back. *Fringe Girl will be there. It's perfect. I got something to tell Keilani, too.*

I typed back: *kk.*

He was in school, so I didn't text him again.

I woke up the following morning feeling anxious about what Alysse and Emily would say about Austin. Did I hope aliens had abducted him? That's what I kept asking myself. Did I want them to tell me that otherworldly beings had called out to him on a wavelength only he could hear? Maybe I did, but only because there was no other explanation for him not aging in five years.

Still, the idea scared me.

Casey showed up at eleven-thirty, Emily and Alysse at noon.

After everyone exchanged pleasantries, Mom turned to me and said, "Time to bring Austin down." Her voice sounded like the frightened whisper of a child hiding under the bed.

Everyone went into the living room while I tromped upstairs to get my brother.

"Austin."

I stood in the doorway to his room. He sat with his legs pulled under him, facing the mirror, drawing away. He was dressed in one of his colorful *Reverse Flash* shirts and short pants (which he'd picked out of his drawer himself.) He didn't look up. The colored pencil made scratching noises on the paper as he filled in details. I entered and squatted down beside him.

"Austin, my friend Emily and her mom are here. And Casey. We're going to have lunch together. You wanna come down with me?"

At first, I thought he would refuse. But he finished filling in the shading on a very life-like pine tree and set his pencil down. Without making eye contact, he stood and waited for me to stand. I did. He turned his head toward the window a moment, as though looking for something. Or was he *listening* for something? I waved him forward and he followed me from the room.

As I slowly descended the stairs, Austin trailing behind, I think I held my breath because I was so nervous. How would Alysse and Emily react to him? I reached the foyer and turned toward the living room.

Everyone stood up as I led Austin forward. "Austin, this is my friend Emily and her mom Alysse."

Of course, he didn't extend a hand. He never did things like that. And they made no attempt to touch him.

"Hi, Austin," Alysse said with a big smile. "It's so nice to finally meet you."

"Yeah, kid," Emily added snidely. "You drove my friend here crazy for five years."

Alysse elbowed her. "Emily!"

She looked slightly ashamed. "Sorry."

I stared aghast at her a long moment, but she wouldn't meet my gaze.

Casey seemed just as confused by Emily's behavior.

I watched Alysse study Austin with great deliberation.

She glanced at Emily. Emily shook her head.

"Well?" That was Mom.

Alysse turned to her. "I don't sense aliens, Leslie."

"Me, either," Emily agreed, her gaze fixed intently on my brother.

Austin didn't seem to care about being the center of attention.

"But there is something...different about him, Mom," Emily added. "Do you sense it?"

Alysse nodded. "Yes. Like his aura has faded a bit."

"Uh, could you two explain what you're talking about?" Dad asked. "I'm lost here."

"So am I," Mom put in. That tremor was back in her voice.

"As we told you before, exposure to aliens affects the auras of human beings," Alysse clarified, "alters them slightly, which is how we always recognize fellow abductees."

"And Austin doesn't have that?"

"No, Tom. But there is something different about his aura. It's almost like he's missing some of it. I've never encountered anything like this before."

"What do you think it means?" Mom's voice quavered and her face scrunched up with renewed fear. She'd been prepared to accept aliens, but now something new had been thrown into the mix and she was clearly panicking.

"I don't know."

I'd been so sure about the abduction theory that having it shot down felt like a punch to the gut.

Alysse turned her gaze from Austin to me. She must've seen my dejection because she stepped forward and drew me into a hug.

"Oh, Colton, I wish I had the answers you need." She held me a long moment and I felt how much she cared for me, which was nice. When she pulled away, she said, "At least we know aliens won't be coming back for him."

I nodded. That was one positive note. There was a long

awkward moment of silence while we all digested this new reality.

"How about we eat? I'm starved."

Everyone turned to Emily.

She shrugged. "I skipped breakfast, okay?"

That broke the frozen moment and Mom said, "Lunch is ready." She led us into the dining room. The table had been set and she invited us to sit. "Alysse, could I ask your help in the kitchen?"

"Of course."

Alysse followed her out of the dining room while the rest of us sat. Austin took his usual seat beside me while Casey took the one on his other side. He did it kind of fast, as though he didn't want Emily sitting there and messing with my brother.

Lunch was pretty chill, I have to say. Somehow knowing that Austin hadn't been abducted by aliens made us all feel more relaxed. Yeah, what Alysse said about his aura was troubling, but she'd eased my mind about anyone or anything returning to snatch him away a second time.

We talked about the Hawaii trip and how much fun it would be to hang out with Keilani. Emily acted dismissive, like she always did. She spent so much time trying to prove she didn't care about anything that it was obvious how much she did. Maybe I just knew her so well by now, but I could tell she wanted to go with us.

I eyed Alysse as I reached for another grilled cheese sandwich (my mom killed it with grilled cheese.) "It would be awesome if you and Emily could vacation with us. Then our whole crew would be together. I mean, I feel like, well, all of this drama with Austin and Kumaka has created a huge family and it'd be so perfect to hang together."

She raised her eyebrows in surprise. "That's a splendid idea, Colton. Em? What do you think?"

Of course, she rolled her eyes. "Leave it to Psycho Boy to get all emotional again."

Alysse frowned. "I told you before I don't like you calling him that."

"I agree," Mom echoed. She'd been in the middle of pouring some lemonade and when she heard Emily call me Psycho Boy, her hand froze in midair, pitcher suspended over the table.

"He likes that name, don't you?" Emily looked across the table at me with assurance in her squinting brown eyes.

I didn't like that name, but didn't want to get her in trouble with her mom. "I guess I'm used to it."

"See?"

"Well, I don't like it and Leslie agrees, so don't use it in my presence."

Alysse glared at Emily, and surprisingly she backed down.

"Oookaaay." Emily drew out the word, like *not* calling people names was the hardest thing in the world for her.

"So whadda ya think, Em?" I asked, wanting to get back to the trip. "All of us in Hawaii together would be lit. Keilani can teach us how to surf."

She rolled her eyes. "Oh, joy, my favorite sport."

"C'mon, Emily," Casey urged. "Hanging out in person will so beat hanging out on Discord."

She looked at the both of us, and then fixed her gaze on Austin for a split second. "Okay."

Dad finally spoke up. "Casey's father and I have been

talking dates and hotels. I'll email you the details, Alysse, and we'll work out the best fit for all of us."

Alysse smiled warmly. "I look forward to it. Can't remember the last time we vacationed anywhere. And with the kids all graduating this year, it'll be perfect."

After lunch, us kids left the grownups to talk grownup stuff and went into Dad's office to call Keilani. I thought Austin would go up to his room like usual, but he trailed after us and sat right next to me. I felt kind of touched by that, as though he knew how upset I'd been by his drawing and wanted to make me feel better.

Keilani was stoked to see us all together, especially with Austin now part of the crew.

"I so wish I could be with you, guys," she gushed. Her hair was damp because she'd already been out for early morning surf practice. "You're seriously my best friends in the world. I mean that and we've never even hung out together in person. It's weird, huh?"

Casey and I exchanged a smile.

"That's about to change, Hawaiian Girl," Emily said with a smirk.

Keilani looked at the camera in confusion.

"Guess who's coming to visit this summer?" I said, unable to keep from grinning.

"Oh, my God, you and Austin?" Her whole face lit up with joy and made her look even more beautiful.

"Yep."

"Fringe Girl and me, too," Casey piped up, unable to contain his excitement. "We'll get to hang together for two whole weeks!"

She screamed. No joke. She actually screamed. "Oh, my God, that is the best graduation present I could ever get! I love you guys!"

"We love you, too," Casey said quickly. "And that's no lie."

He made it sound like a flippant line, but I knew Casey better than anyone and I heard the underlying urgency in his tone. I also knew what he was about to do.

"Uh, Keilani." Casey hesitated. I'd never seen him look so insecure. "I want you to see something."

Keilani looked confused. "Sure."

Casey reached into the manila envelope he'd brought from home and slipped out a plane ticket. He held it up to the camera.

Keilani leaned in and squinted to read the ticket on her screen. "A plane ticket?"

Casey nodded and slowly turned it over. On the back, in large letters, he'd written with a sharpie: *Will you go to prom with me?*

She gasped. Big time. She threw a hand to her mouth the way my mom sometimes did. But she didn't say anything.

Casey crumbled a bit, while Emily muttered, "Oh, brother."

"Uh, I have a ticket for your mom, too," Casey went on quickly. It was obvious he believed she was about to say no. "I know you have a boyfriend and all, but we really never had a chance to get to know each other and my parents think it would be awesome and I, well, I just wish you'd say yes."

She lowered her hand and her eyes welled with tears. "Of course, I want to go to prom with you," she gushed with excitement. "I just never thought it was possible."

180

Casey broke into the biggest grin ever. "That's...wow! You just made my whole life."

Emily shook her head in derision. "Cute Boy becomes the typical YA novel hyperbolic teen. Yuck!"

Neither Keilani nor Casey even acknowledged her comment. They were too happy. And so was I. Hell, I was a hyperbolic teen, too.

"What about your boyfriend?" Emily asked Keilani, as though she was determined to spoil the mood.

"What boyfriend?" Keilani wiped her eyes with some tissue.

"Duh! The one on your Facebook status where it says, 'in a relationship'?"

Casey frowned, and I saw the worry on his face.

"Now who's going all teen novel?" Keilani said to Emily. "I put that there so the boys at school wouldn't bug me. I told them I had a boyfriend at another school."

"Uh, where?" Casey asked, his voice sounding kind of small, without his usual timber.

She grinned. "Tamalpais High."

I got it right away, but it took Casey a moment to under-stand. Once he did, he broke into a smile that filled up his whole face.

"Too much subterfuge and game playing for me," Emily said with a snort. "Here's how you invite someone to prom. Colton, I'm going to your prom with you. Mine will suck big time and I don't like anyone at my school anyway."

My eyebrows shot up in surprise and I opened my mouth to speak, but she plowed on.

"The way I see it, all the girls at your school will fall all over you about how moved they were—" She threw her hands across her heart dramatically. "—and how your tearful confession made them weep with remorse for all the bad things they said to you over the years, and then the phony females will swarm around you hoping for a prom invite. I'm protecting you from those vultures. With me, you're safe. You know I'm legit."

I had my mouth open in shock and so did Casey. I honestly had no clue what to say, so I just stared, looking like a fool.

"Well?" Emily asked, arching her eyebrows. "You don't get an invite like that very often."

Keilani chuckled. "That's very true, Colton."

I hadn't planned on going to prom. Dancing wasn't my thing and I had no one to go with.

"Come on, Colt," Casey urged with a punch to the shoulder. "It'll be perfect, us all together like that."

I gazed at Emily as sternly as I could. I felt I had to assert myself somehow. "I won't dance."

She rolled her eyes. "Like you could?"

I leaned back from the computer. "Can you?"

She shrugged. "Technically, no. But that's beside the point."

Keilani said, "Please, Colton? I really want you there. Casey's right, it'll be so perfect."

I felt like I was being talked into something I didn't want to do, but then I thought of my parents. They'd be thrilled to see me do something "typical" for a change. And Keilani was right. The four of us together would be epic.

"Okay, I'll go with you to *my* prom," I told Emily, and she offered a grin in reply.

Keilani clapped loudly and then we all chatted about what

colors the girls would wear so us guys could get tuxes that matched.

Austin sat beside me the entire time and looked like he was following the conversation. After everyone went home, he waited for me to go upstairs with him. Then he stood at the window and gazed out at the woods. I walked up to his side, gazed at the blue sky and green trees, and felt wistful. Sure, things were looking good for a change. Even if we never learned the truth about him, Austin was home and that was what mattered. Casey found out Keilani liked him, I had a date to prom (if one could call Emily a date—she wanted me to dress like Count Dracula), and the four of us who'd come together through tragedy had become the best of friends.

But I still felt sad as I turned my gaze from the natural beauty outside and fixed it onto my ageless, silent brother.

"I'd give up anything to know what you're thinking."

I didn't expect an answer. But he kind of gave me one. He turned and locked eyes with mine. That was the best I was going to get.

I think Emily really did get psychic powers from those aliens. Or maybe, despite her hard-ass demeanor, she just understood teenage girls. But she'd nailed it.

School on Monday was almost scary for how different it felt. I walked in with Casey and tried to keep a low profile, but girls came out of the woodwork to gush over my interview and how it made them cry. They all had confessions, like, "I apologized to my mom for what I said," or "I made things right with my brother because of what you said." I heard declarations like that all day. Even some of the guys complimented me, saying I looked like a loser for crying on camera, but that I made them think about what they'd said to other people.

And most importantly of all, the other kids finally understood why I'd acted so crazy since middle school. Maybe it was because of that saying, "until you walk in my shoes ...," but my old nickname, "Psycho Boy," wasn't uttered once the entire day. It's hard for me to describe how I felt, but "liberated" comes close. It was like I'd been wearing a costume all those years and finally ditched it for my own clothes. Or maybe I was shedding my old skin for a new one. Whatever it was, for the first time I could recall, I didn't hate being at school.

Over those next few days, Emily's other words proved prescient, too. Girls I barely knew hinted they were available for prom, and I was super glad she'd already invited me. Better the devil you know, right?

Seriously, everything looked brighter than ever. I'd even been accepted to several art colleges.

But then the rain returned to Mill Valley, and my life forever changed.

Chapter 13

Can't I Come with You?

Mom told me that since I've been back at school, Austin would either draw or stand at the window all day but always knew the exact moment I entered the house. It was kind of eerie.

Every day after school, he'd show me new artwork in which I had blond hair and Mom had red. Sometimes there was a rainbow in the background; other drawings had shimmering splashes of colored light like in the first one he'd shown me. But always, towering trees surrounded us. I studied each drawing intently but came up empty. I'd shown them to Mom and Dad, and they were just as mystified, though Mom did mention that she'd thought about dying her hair red but had dropped the idea after Austin vanished. How weird!

I also showed the drawings to Casey and the crew, but no one could make sense of them.

"We may never know the answer, Cry Boy," Emily said. I

185

guess what our moms had said about her name-calling had an impact, because she'd quickly changed my nickname. "Because you cry so well on camera." she'd asserted.

I think I liked "Psycho Boy" better.

"Maybe you should just let it go, Colton," Keilani said quietly, her voice hitching with emotion. "You have him back."

I felt terrible, realizing she might never see Kumaka again. "You're right."

The next morning, I woke up to the sound of rainfall. I felt anxious the second I heard it but didn't know why. Maybe I still believed it was the rain that had spirited Austin away the first time, or maybe it was because the last time it rained, Austin came home. I sat bolt upright in my sleeping bag to find Austin at the window in his pajamas staring at the downpour. I clambered out of the bag and went to him. The rain seemed heavy, but it was February and rain was normal for that time of year.

I was about to head into the bathroom to get ready for school when Austin turned and grabbed my arm. He held on tight.

I looked into his eyes and my heart hammered with dread. He was pointing out at the rain, just as he had the day he vanished. His eyes locked on mine, but, like always, they held no obvious message. Still, he *was* telling me something.

More than ever before, I wanted to scream with frustration at my inability to communicate with my brother. When I told Mom I didn't want to go to school because of what Austin did, we both went to his room to check on him. He still stood by the window. He allowed me to dress him in long pants and a long sleeve pullover shirt, but as soon as I finished, he returned to the window and planted himself like a tree.

The weird drawings and the rain pelting hard against the roof combined to set my nerves on edge. I felt like the house was under attack. Mom seemed unnerved, too, and agreed to let me stay with Austin. It was just as well. No way could I have concentrated on schoolwork.

It was midafternoon and I'd been sitting at Austin's desk, struggling to write a coherent essay for British Lit while Austin remained by the window. The heaviest rain had abated and now there were just light showers. Patches of blue peeked out from behind thick clouds, and it looked like the main body of the storm had passed. I hoped so. I suspected I wouldn't feel safe again until the rain stopped completely.

Mom had left for the store and Dad was at the office, so it was just Austin and me in the house. I pushed back from the desk and stood to stretch. I told Austin I needed to use the bathroom and slipped out of his room. He never even glanced my way.

I was only gone a few minutes, but when I stepped back into the room, it was empty. I nearly choked with terror. Something drew my gaze toward the window, and I froze. A huge rainbow arched across the sky, dipping down into the woods of Mount Tam.

Oh, no....

I bolted from the room and down the stairs. The front door hung open. My chest pulled tight, and I hesitated for a split second in the foyer. I strode forward and looked out into the driveway.

Austin stood beneath the dwindling rain showers, waiting for me. When I leaped off the porch to the paved driveway, he turned to walk down the drive toward the street. I trotted along

187

beside him, urging him to return to the house. But he kept walking.

I considered calling Mom on my cell, but he was moving at a steady pace, and I didn't want to fumble with my phone in the rain. I shivered more from the weirdness of his behavior than the damp, cool air and stayed by his side as he marched boldly up Marin View Avenue to Panoramic Highway.

He didn't hesitate. He tromped across the empty highway and started down the path toward the woods. I flanked him the whole way. The sky was beginning to clear and though the ocean in the distance looked choppy, it was calmer than it had been at the height of the storm. The air felt chilly and neither of us wore a jacket. I shivered again, but Austin seemed oblivious to the cold.

He didn't once turn his head to acknowledge me, but he didn't try to ditch me, either. When I looked ahead to figure out where he was going, my heartbeat quickened with dread. He was heading straight for that spectacular rainbow! Had I been right before? Is this what he'd done when he ran away?

But no one can find the end of a rainbow, my frantic mind screamed at me. I'd tried when Austin first vanished, but it wasn't possible! A rainbow is just refracted light.

I guess no one told Austin that because he followed the paved path until it veered away from the rainbow and then he stopped at the edge of the woods, his gaze fixed straight ahead. I stopped at his side. The rain had nearly ceased, and the rainbow shone bright and colorful in the blue sky overhead.

I fought back panic as I waited to see what he would do next. He tilted his head slightly as though he heard something. I listened, but there were no sounds except scattered raindrops striking the ground and the occasional chirping of birds in the distance.

Austin turned to me and did something that sent my heart into my throat. He extended a hand. I almost gagged. What was going on? Trembling with fear, I let him grasp my hand. He stepped off the path and pulled me into the woods.

This was the west face of Mount Tam; I recognized the sloping terrain and specific trees from my previous visits. I probably knew those trees better than I knew anyone at Tamalpais High. I couldn't even remember the number of times I'd taken this same route. But there was nothing out here *except* trees, so where was Austin leading me?

The rainbow loomed before us. But this time, rather than never getting any closer—like all the times I'd tried to reach one —it grew larger by the minute, sparkling with life and light as the rain became a drizzle.

Austin never looked back. With my hand firmly in his, he pulled me steadily along. My heart pumped with expectation—and trepidation. Normally, the intoxicating aroma of the forest calmed my soul.

Not today.

The rainbow filled my field of vision as we approached a clearing I knew all too well. I'd spent many hours there over the past five years, contemplating my mistakes and thinking about the brother I'd lost.

But there's nothing in that clearing, I thought. *Why is Austin going there?*

I couldn't pull out my phone to check the time, so I didn't know how long we'd been walking when we stepped into the empty clearing and Austin stopped.

Except it wasn't empty.

Not quite.

Eddies of light shimmered at the edges of my vision. Droplets of color, almost. They seemed to fill the clearing, and yet they didn't. And the area *felt* different. Having spent so much time here, I knew that clearing as well as I knew my own bedroom.

Tall, thick trees surrounded us on all sides, but the open space in the middle was just grass and brush, as though nature had cleared a spot for animals to conduct meetings. It had always felt peaceful and solitary.

Not today.

Still peaceful, yes, but not solitary.

We weren't alone.

I instinctively knew others were there and that made my skin crawl. Why couldn't I see them?

Austin stepped forward with deliberation and pulled me gently with him. My breathing slowed and my heart felt like machine-gun fire in my chest.

Austin took several more steps and stopped. He turned and I gasped. His eyes were no longer expressionless. They danced with joy. And then he did something else he never had before—he smiled.

"This is where I went, Colton," he said and I lurched back in shock, letting go of his hand and stumbling away from him.

Surprised by my reaction, Austin stepped toward me again. His face went slack and emotionless—the way it had always looked. He reached out a hand.

I could scarcely breathe. What was happening here?

I lifted one trembling arm and let him take my hand again.

He backed up and his face once again returned to animated life. Then he took a few more steps back and pulled me forward. I shuddered as something passed through me. It was what I imagined a ghost would feel like if one passed through my body.

"I'm sorry, Colton," Austin offered with a shy grin. "I didn't mean to scare you."

I felt my emotions rise and a thousand questions bubble to the surface. But it was like I no longer had control over my body. My mind was active. I knew what I felt and wanted to say, but I couldn't speak. My voice wouldn't work. I panicked but couldn't even express that.

Austin eased me back a few steps. "Keep your left foot right there."

He stopped pushing and suddenly, I could talk again. "Oh, God, what happened to me?"

"It's because your brain was made for your dimension, Colton. In this one, you're like I was over there."

I felt light-headed. No joke. I thought I would faint. "You can talk!"

Austin laughed. It was a hearty laugh, and his voice was strong and deep. "I can here, but over there, I could only think what I wanted to say."

I stared at him as though I'd never seen him before. And I hadn't. This Austin was alive and vibrant and...happy. He brushed damp hair from in front of his eyes and gazed at me with obvious love.

"There's so much I wanna tell you, Colton." His happiness drooped. "But we don't have much time."

My breath hitched. "What do you mean?" But then I knew. "You're leaving again?"

He nodded.

"Please don't go, Austin," I pleaded. "I'm sorry for what I said. I didn't mean it. Really. I never hated you!"

"I know. That's what I've been trying to tell you ever since I got back, especially with my drawings, but I just confused you more." He paused and his face clouded over with guilt.

That fainting feeling came over me again. Was this really happening or was I imagining it all?

"How come you never talked if you could?"

"My brain wouldn't let me. This is going to sound crazy, I know, but I...I should've been born in *this* dimension, not the one I grew up in."

There was that word again. "Dimension?" My head spun with confusion.

He shrugged. "I only learned a little in the time I was here, but this is like a reverse dimension of yours, kind of like folding paper in two and cutting out a shape in the crease. When you open the paper, you have mirror images."

Mirror images?

"You mean there's another world besides this one?"

"I think it's more of a parallel dimension in the same world."

My brain fought to comprehend these incredible revelations. And then a terrifying thought hit me. "Is there another version of everyone over there?"

He nodded, biting his lip, as though knowing what I was about to say next.

"Including me?"

"Yes, Colton. I only talked to the other you for a little while. You look, well, different, but kinda the same. Mom and Dad, too."

I felt light-headed and fought to keep my balance. "What about you?"

He frowned, his soft features darkening with sadness. "The version of me that should've been born in your dimension was born here, by mistake. Somehow, the dimensions overlapped, and we flipped. I guess it happens once in a while. It's weird, I know."

He stopped talking, the sadness spreading more deeply over his face and dimming his vibrant eyes.

Almost afraid to ask, I muttered, "Uh, what happened to the other Austin?"

He stiffened. "They told me...he died."

Sadness overwhelmed me, an endless sea of loss for a brother I never even knew. And yet, I did have a brother, and he was standing right before me!

"This can't be true. *You're* my brother."

"It explains a lot about me, Colton. My brain sort of works in reverse over there, which is why I couldn't talk out loud, why I needed mirrors around, why I always drew everything backwards, even why I liked those *Reverse Flash* and *Bizarro* comics more than the regular ones. In this dimension, everything is the flip side of over there."

I looked around. Other than those shimmering drops of color filling my peripheral vision, I saw nothing but the clearing. "Where are we now, exactly?"

"You could call it the end of the rainbow, I guess."

I flinched. "That's impossible. No one can find the end of a rainbow."

"When colors are visible, like in Dr. Loftus's office or in rainbows, I can hear the light. It took me a long time and a lot of listening, but I finally heard it really strong that day I left the house. This light we're in now, this particular kind of rainbow, it's like a doorway connecting the two dimensions."

My mind reeled. None of this was possible, was it? My science teachers would say no one could hear the colors of light. But then I recalled what Agent Martin said about Austin being able to hear at frequencies most people couldn't.

"Well, um, why do you look the same as before?" I felt like my brain would snap trying to make sense of all these revelations.

"Oh, I think that's because a rainbow is light, and time moves slower at the speed of light. I learned that from those science shows I used to watch. I stayed mostly in the doorway the whole time, so I was between dimensions, I guess. I freaked out that five years went by for you."

"But–"

"Colton," Austin interrupted. "My time is running out."

My head kept spinning in circles. "Why?"

The colors flickered and Austin glanced around with concern. "Because I'm going to stay here this time, with the other version of my family."

"No. You belong with me and Mom and Dad. *We're* your family."

Austin placed both hands gently on my shoulders. "Yes, Colton, you are my brother, and you always will be. I barely know the other Colton or my parents over here, but I want to have a regular life that I can't have with you."

This was all too much, and I bit back a scream of frustration. "Show me. I can't let you go until I see for myself."

194

"I can only give you a quick peek, Colton. The rainbow's fading and when it does, the doorway will close."

"Okay."

"You're going to feel like you did before, when you couldn't talk or react, so don't freak out."

I nodded and steeled myself for that complete lack of control that made my brain feel like it was wrapped in cellophane.

Austin tugged gently on my shoulders, and I lurched forward two steps. That feeling of being trapped inside myself slammed trough my brain and I screamed a silent wail of anguish as he let me go.

Standing twenty feet away, looking like he'd seen a ghost, was...me! The mirror image of myself stared across the clearing, gazing in open-mouthed wonder. So did the two people flanking him. They looked identical to my parents...except they didn't. Mom had long red hair and Dad...was that a cop uniform he wore? My dad, a cop? Then I took in the other me. He had straight blond hair, not black and anime-style like mine, and he wore some kind of preppy school uniform. And he looked my current age, gazing at me in open-mouthed shock.

Now I understood Austin's drawings! He'd been trying to show me this alternate version of us. I stared in astonishment at this other family and my inability to express my feelings in words made me feel like I'd explode any moment.

The alternate version of my mom nudged the other me, and he stepped closer, but stayed outside the sparkles of light. He looked shy and nervous, rubbing his hands on his pants.

"Hey, Colton," he said, his voice deep and strong. Did I sound like that? "I know you can't talk, but I, uh, I just wanna thank you. Austin told us you always stood up for him and got in tons of trouble defending him when kids called him names. And he told us he could see you searching for him when he was here with us. I hope I would've done the same."

For the first time I truly understood Austin's frustration growing up. There was so much I wanted to say to this other me. My brain screamed with frustration. But all I could do was listen.

"I just want you to know that we'll take good care of Austin. I'll never be as badass as you, but my parents are cool, and they'll love him like they do me."

I looked past him at his parents. His mom was crying and his dad had one arm around her. So much like my own mom and dad.

The droplets of colored light flickered around me. The other Colton noticed too.

"I've done a lot of searching on the internet here," he went on, faster than before, "and I think the government knows about this whole dimension thing. Yours does too, probably. Maybe scientists will figure out some way we can visit each other for real. Anyway, it's been cool meeting you."

He raised a hand in farewell.

Then I felt a gentle push backwards, the cellophane around my mind lifted with a jolting suddenness, and I could speak once again.

"I...can't...believe it!" I gasped. The clearing behind Austin was empty once again.

"I didn't either, at first," Austin replied, removing his hands from my shoulders. "I'm sure Kumaka's here, too, with his other family. I felt him the last time I came, even though he must've been in Hawaii. That's why I held onto that picture of him you showed me."

Another flicker of light shifted the air around us.

"I only have a few more minutes," Austin continued, his soft features exuding tenderness. "I came back because I wanted you to know I forgave you. I didn't mean to diss Mom and Dad, but I kind of latched onto you because I didn't have all the mirrors like I did before. You were my anchor over there." He glanced down and his cheeks bloomed red. "You were always my anchor, Colton, even when I knew you were mad at me. When I saw you searching for me, that meant the world."

My brain felt thick and my body tight. "You saw me?"

He nodded. "Yeah. I'm super stubborn like you, 'cause I stayed in the doorway watching you, so I never became totally part of that other dimension. I guess I was there longer than it felt to me. Maybe that's why Alysse said my aura looked faded."

I nodded as tears dribbled out and mixed with the drizzling rain misting my face.

He stepped closer and looked me right in the eye, but unlike most of my life when there'd been nothing in that gaze, this time I saw his soul. I saw the pain he felt at having to leave, but also the intense need.

"I need to stay, Colton. I hope you understand. And can help Mom and Dad understand. I would've brought them, too, but you were the only one at home when the rainbow showed up."

I gasped. I'd completely forgotten about Mom. Without moving my leg, I reached into my pants pocket and slipped out my phone. No bars. Course not in the middle of a forest!

Austin seemed to read my thoughts and indicated the

phone. "We can take some selfies. And you can record me giving them a message."

I nodded numbly.

"Do you understand why I need to leave?" Austin's soft brown eyes widened with fear, like I might yell at him or something. "Do you think I'm being selfish?"

"I don't think you're selfish." I knew, now, how hard his inner life must've been all those years. "It sounds like you're just going back to where you were always supposed to be." I tried for a smile, but so much sadness filled me that I'm sure it looked like a grimace.

"Thanks, Colton." Austin moved closer so we were side by side.

I didn't do anything.

He gently lifted my arm so the phone faced us. "C'mon, little brother, don't be shy."

It was almost funny how our relationship had changed in a heartbeat. I activated the selfie camera.

Austin nudged me. "Smile, Colton."

I did, despite my teary eyes, and snapped off a few shots. Austin crowded in to view the pictures. Seeing the image of my brother so energetic and alive and filled with joy made me shudder. I almost dropped the phone. He grabbed my hand.

"I know this is super freaky for you, Colton. Me, too. But I want you to be happy."

"How?" I choked. More tears fell. I didn't fight them. I didn't even feel embarrassed. I just let them tumble out and gazed at my brother through blurred vision. "How can I be happy when I won't ever see you again?"

He offered me another tender smile. How I loved that smile and the glint of life in his eyes.

"Every time you see a really bright rainbow, I'll be there, right on the other side."

"Yeah?" My heart pounded with hope.

"Yeah."

My field of vision shimmered and faded slightly.

"Hurry, Colton," Austin said as he stepped out in front of me. "Put on the video record."

I did and pointed the phone at him.

"Hi Mom and Dad," Austin began, flashing that shy look again. "I only have a few, so I'll be super quick. Colton can tell you the rest. I just want you to know I'm safe and happy and I wanna thank you for everything you did for me. I couldn't have asked for better parents. I wish I could hug you, but I can't. Just don't forget that I miss you and I'll always love you." The color droplets twinkled again, and Austin hurried to me. "The doorway is closing."

I wanted more. I didn't want him to leave. Not now. Not when I was just getting to know my brother. "Can't I come with you? I can leave the phone here for Mom and Dad to find."

Austin shook his head.

"Why not?"

"There's *already* a version of you here." He gripped my hands and squeezed. "This is where *I* belong, Colton. You belong in your dimension with Mom and Dad. They need you." That shy smile crept back onto his face. "I'll miss you more than anyone." Tears welled in his eyes. "Have a happy life, little brother."

He leaned in and hugged me tightly. I was crying outright as I threw my arms around him and pulled him in close.

"I love you, Austin," I choked, barely able to articulate the words. "I always have."

"I love you, too," he sniffled as he pulled back from the hug. "Best *big* little brother a kid could ask for."

Despite my pain, I smiled.

Austin stepped back a few feet and grinned through his tears. "You can film me if you want. Might look super cool."

I raised the camera and activated the video. My whole body shook with sorrow. I had to fight the urge to run and grab him in another hug.

He must've sensed my temptation because he said, "Don't move. Long as you have one foot in your dimension, you'll stay."

I nodded. I was sobbing now and fought to keep the camera steady.

The outline of Austin's entire body sparkled with color, his aura glowing. He flickered like a star in the night sky, then faded slightly and returned, radiant and lustrous. I felt the air shimmer and shift around me, the colors at the edges of my vision flitting in and out of focus.

"Remember, Colton, whenever you see a rainbow, I'll be there."

And then he was gone. The sky above the trees was blue with scattered clouds. The rainbow had vanished, taking that other dimension—and my brother—with it.

I dropped to my knees and wept.

I must've stayed like that for hours, crying and thinking and regretting, feeling every emotion it was possible to feel. By the time I got home, it was much later than I thought, and I was a basket case. Mom and Dad were there, and they'd called the cops again, of course. Mom was so happy to see me she threw her arms around me and just held on. I couldn't speak. I cried and she kept me close, and Dad put one hand on my shoulder, and they didn't pepper me with questions, for which I was grateful.

I finally collected myself enough to pull the phone from my pocket and hand it to Mom. My wallpaper was the selfie of Austin and me in the clearing. She eyed it uncertainly.

"Colton, where's Austin?"

I nearly let loose another torrent of tears but held it together. Police were hovering around, so I didn't want to be too loud. "He said to tell you he loves you."

Dad made a kind of gagging sound.

"Watch the videos," I said and then couldn't handle anything more. I ran past them into the house and collapsed onto my bed. Once again, I cried myself to sleep.

The video of Austin disappearing was pretty badass, I have to say, and that selfie will be on my home screen forever. I guess because of our fringy investigations over the years, none of us totally freaked out that a mirror dimension with alternate versions of ourselves existed, though none of us pretended to understand the science of it.

Mom cried for a long time; Dad, too. Losing Austin so soon after getting him back was devastating, but after a few hours of bonding through our mutual grief, we all agreed that Austin's happiness was more important than what we wanted.

Dad tried to lighten the mood by saying, "Me, a cop? Hard to believe." But then his face became thoughtful. "Course, like most kids, I wanted to be a cop when I was young. Funny how that worked out over there."

Mom hadn't said much, but at least she'd stopped crying. "I'm glad he's still here and not off with aliens somewhere."

My mind had been awhirl with questions and wonderings about that other dimension ever since I got home. "It's like he's in another Mill Valley side by side with this one. The clearing over there looked exactly like the one in our woods. I can almost feel him here in this room with us right now."

Mom studied me a long moment and then pulled me into a tight hug. We were all seated on the couch close together and had been hugging more than I can ever remember.

"Thank you for saying that, Colton. It makes me feel a bit better." Then she offered a small smile. "I can't picture you blond and wearing preppy clothes, though."

I smiled for the first time. "Me, either."

"How did it feel to meet, well, yourself?" Dad was studying me with raised eyebrows.

"Freaky," I answered. Then I turned to Mom on my other side. "But you look good with red hair, Mom."

She smiled again and pulled me into another hug. Dad joined in and we just sat like that for who knew how long. Despite losing Austin, I'd never felt closer to my family than I did at that moment.

After further discussion, we decided not to share the video with the world. Yeah, there were tons of questions, and the authorities interviewed me multiple times, just like before. But I stuck to my story that I went to the bathroom and when I came back, Austin was gone. Like before, there was no evidence of foul play and no sign of him anywhere.

Why didn't we show them—and the media—the video of Austin fading away? What good would that have done? Would they have believed my story about a parallel dimension? Unlikely. They'd come up with all kinds of explanations for the video—like AI software—and we'd be under more suspicion than ever regarding Austin's disappearance.

Mom also feared that telling the world about another dimension might be even worse than being an abductee. It would freak out those people who believed it, and *we'd* have paparazzi and scientists descending on us like locusts. We'd never know another moment's privacy, and she felt our family had already had more than enough drama for one lifetime.

I did suggest that we show Agents Martin and Spencer the video. "I'm sure they'd believe me, especially Agent Martin."

"They'd have to share your story with the government and then we're back to where we started," Dad said after a few moments.

"They might know about it already," I said, recalling what Alysse said about that Hadron Collider thing and what the "other" Colton said about his government. "We could ask the agents to not tell where they got the information. Maybe I shouldn't, but I trust them."

Dad and Mom said they would consider the idea, but not until everything settled down.

Of course, the media returned in force, but I only gave them one statement, without cussing this time.

"I never understood my brother and I resented him for being different. Now I know how much he wanted to communicate with us. He just couldn't. Don't ask me how I know; I just do. I love him more than anyone in the world and when I'm older, I wanna work with kids just like him."

Later that evening, Anderson Cooper called me on my cell to ask how I was holding up.

"I'm good, CNN Dude," I said, hoping his nickname would assure him I was telling the truth. "I wish I could tell you why, but I know Austin is happy, so I'm happy."

He didn't press me for information. Instead, he offered to buy three of my paintings for a thousand dollars each. I almost dropped the phone. "You can use the money to help kids like Austin, like you said on the news."

Overwhelmed with gratitude, I gushingly thanked him.

"Hey, what are CNN Dudes for?"

I laughed. "Thanks so much."

"Keep in touch, Colton. You're going to do great things in life. I can tell."

I felt pumped up with pride upon ending the call.

Casey came by that night and did something he never had before—he hugged me. "Sure you're okay, Colt?"

I pulled away and nodded. Of course, I showed him the video and told him everything. Like my parents and me, he didn't freak out about the other dimension – I guess we'd all been through too much to question anything anymore. He expressed curiosity about what his mirror self might be like but accepted the alternate dimension reality with relative ease.

He teared up as he watched Austin's message to Mom and Dad. "Damn, man."

We sat a moment in silence when it ended. Then I told him what Austin said about Kumaka. He looked both happy and sad, and I understood why. Happy because Kumaka was safe, but sad because Keilani would never see him again.

We called her. She had already seen the news and had been trying to contact *me*, but this was the first opportunity I'd had to get online.

"Oh, God, Colton, I'm so sorry! Are you okay?"

She looked so worried that my heart thumped wildly. "Yeah, Keilani, I'm good."

I told her what happened, and about Kumaka. She listened in stoic silence, then broke down and sobbed.

"It's okay, Keilani," Casey blurted, his voice filled with empathy. "Austin said he's probably fine over there."

She nodded but couldn't speak. Rather than force her, I played the videos from my phone. She gasped when she heard Austin speak and made a kind of choking sound when he vanished.

As I watched the vids and thought over everything that had happened in that clearing, it finally struck me that Austin had used my favorite adjective while talking to me—super. The realization made me feel good, like my brother had taken a small part of me into his new world, and I felt more connected to him than ever.

The videos ended and we three sat in silence, digesting the emotions I knew were swirling around all our hearts and minds. I'd thought of including Emily but was afraid she might say something inappropriate that would hurt Keilani. I'd call her later.

"Thank you, Colton," Keilani whispered, her voice raw and strained, almost like she had a sore throat. "It's unbelievable that there's another dimension overlapping ours, but I guess I shouldn't be surprised after all we've learned these past five years." She paused a moment and bit her lip absently in thought. "I hope my...well, my other self is taking good care of him."

"I'm sure she is," I said, my own voice struggling to stay steady.

Keilani's face clouded over with curiosity. "And I wish we knew what happened to *our* Kumaka."

"Me, too," Casey agreed.

Keilani signed off to go tell her mom.

I didn't think any day could be as difficult as the one when Austin disappeared the first time, but this one had outdone it.

Casey and I sat staring at the selfie of Austin and me, which was now my desktop image.

"He looks happy, Colt."

"He is."

It had been a month since Austin left for the second, and final, time. At school, kids expressed sympathy that he'd vanished again, rather than suspicion and enmity like before. Somehow, I'd become someone *in* pain, rather than someone who *caused* pain. Maybe it was because all of us were older now and had learned something about empathy. Or maybe it was because of what I'd said on Anderson Cooper's show, but I was no longer the outcast. I was someone other kids sought out for advice because, I guess, they figured I'd been through it and would understand.

I also realized that I'd pushed people away when I was

younger, kids who might have been sympathetic back when everything first happened. Funny how life works. I used to resent my brother for being trapped inside himself and yet I trapped myself and made others resent *me* for it. Life is circular, I guess.

It had rained for the past two days, and I was on heightened alert. Rain meant a rainbow and a rainbow meant Austin. Casey was walking with me down the hallway after school. The rain had turned to a drizzle and my heart pounded with expectation. Casey chattered on about prom and how excited he was to finally see Keilani in person and how I shouldn't let Emily dress me up as Dracula, no matter how much she insisted.

But my gaze kept flitting to the windows. And finally, I saw it. A magnificent rainbow appeared in the pale blue sky outside, refracting through the window glass into myriad colors. I sprinted for the doors.

"Colt!"

I didn't stop. I heard Casey chasing after me. I spotted kids giving me funny looks, but I ignored them.

I shoved the doors wide and leaped down the concrete steps to the parking lot. Some kids milled about while others moved toward their cars. I ignored them. My gaze remained fixed on that shimmering rainbow overhead.

He was over there somewhere.

I grinned and raised a hand to wave. "Hi, Austin. I hope you're happy over there."

Kids gawked. I saw them in my peripheral vision. I felt a hand on my shoulder and knew it was Casey.

"You okay, man?"

I nodded, my face one giant smile. "Never better." I turned

and clapped him on the back. "Wanna come over and hang out? We can talk prom stuff."

He grinned. "Course."

I threw one arm around his shoulders and led the way to my car.

I was finally at peace.

Thank you, Austin.

THE END

About the Author

Michael J. Bowler is the award-winning author of A MATTER OF TIME, THE LANCE CHRONICLES, THE HEALER CHRONICLES, THE FILM MILIEU THRILLER SERIES, THE INVICTUS CHRONICLES, FOREVER BOY, and LOSING AUSTIN.

His screenplay, "THE GOD MACHINE," won First Place in the 2017 Scriptapalooza competition and in the 2023 Tarzana International Film Festival.

He grew up in San Rafael, California. He worked as producer, writer, and/or director on several ultra-low-budget horror films, including "Hell Spa," "Fatal Images," "Club Dead," and "Things II."

He taught high school in Hawthorne, California—both in general education and to students with learning disabilities—in subjects ranging from English and Strength Training to Algebra, Biology, and Yearbook.

He has been a volunteer Big Brother to eight different boys with the Catholic Big Brothers Big Sisters program, a decades-long volunteer within the juvenile justice system in Los Angeles and is a single dad to an adopted child.

He has been honored as Probation Volunteer of the Year, YMCA Volunteer of the Year, California Big Brother of the

Year, and National Big Brother of the Year. The "National" honor allowed him and three of his Little Brothers to visit the White House and meet the president in the Oval Office.

Website: michaeljbowler.com
FB: michaeljbowlerauthor
Twitter: @MichaelJBowler
Instagram: @michaeljbowler
Pinterest: http://www.pinterest.com/michaelbowler/pins/
YouTube: https://www.youtube.com/channel/
UC2NXCPry4DDgJZOVDUxVtMw

Join my mailing list at MichaelJBowler.com for updates on upcoming releases and free reads.

facebook.com/michaeljbowlerauthor
x.com/MichaelJBowler
instagram.com/MichaelJBowler

Excerpt from FOREVER BOY

Here's an Excerpt from My
Multi-Award-Winning
FOREVER BOY

As he entered his bedroom, he heard a gasp behind him and turned to find Stephanie staring in awe at the various horror film posters blanketing his walls. He'd been afraid she'd laugh, but instead she was grinning.

"This is the most amazing room I've ever been in!" she gushed, her head swiveling from one wall to the next. "I've seen every one of these movies."

"Wait... what? You like horror movies?"

"Who doesn't?" Her gaze settled on the shelves filled with his models, and she practically leaped forward, sweeping over each with her eyes as though soaking up water in a desert. "Did you make these? Sorry, stupid question, of course you did. May I?"

He nodded and she reverently picked up the figure of Dracula in a graveyard, encircling himself with his cape, blood dripping from his fangs.

"The detail work," she muttered, scrutinizing it, "the craftsmanship. You're the geek of all geeks."

"Thanks," he mumbled, sarcasm saturating his voice.

She spun around, grinning. "Oh, I meant that in a good way."

Honestly, even at school with her friends, Isaac had never seen her look so animated, so...happy.

As though handling the crown jewels, she set the figure back onto its shelf and stepped back. "I have a thing for vampires. They seem so sexy."

"If you say so."

She spotted his book collection, all horror titles. "Whoa, you like Stephen King too?"

"Course. He's the greatest horror writer in the last hundred years. In fact, I'm making a short horror film to enter a competition in Bangor over Halloween weekend. King will be one of the judges."

Her face lit up. "That's awesome. Who's acting in it?"

"Only Drágan so far. I need a female lead and a few others."

"I could do it," she blurted. "I was in the school play last year."

He squinted at her with suspicion. "Sure you don't just wanna be around Drágan? There's no kissing scenes."

She flinched, clearly offended. "You sound like my lousy, stinking pig of a stepfather."

He bowed his head. "Sorry. Would you really be in my film?"

"And get a chance to meet Stephen King? Of course!"

"Um, well, great. I'm just revising the script, but I can get it to you this week."

"I can't wait." She paused, gazing at him so intently he squirmed. "You and I have so much in common, I never knew."

He attempted a flippant tone. "Since we never talk, I guess it's hard to find these things out."

Her grin fell away, replaced by a look of shame. "I'm sorry. You know how it is at school. The popular kids and the..."

She trailed off, but he finished for her. "The losers, like me."

"Except you're not, but..."

"But you still can't talk to me at school. I get it. I can email you the script."

"Awesome!" She recited her email address and Isaac put it into his phone.

"So, what'd you wanna talk to me about? If it's Drágan you came for, he's gone."

"I know. I've been watching your house all morning, hoping he might leave."

He furrowed his brows. "Why?"

"To show you these." She crossed the room on her long, athletic legs and set her messenger bag on his desk. Flipping it open, she extracted what looked like a bundle of large photos. "Remember I took those pics of Drágan yesterday?"

"Yeah, so?"

"Since you said he was a model, I uploaded one of them and did an internet search."

Isaac was growing impatient. "And you found out he's not a model?"

She shook her head, shoving the length of her hair back over one shoulder. "He's a model, all right, but check out these pictures. I wrote the dates at the bottom, like when each one first showed up in print."

She handed him the stack of photos. The top image nearly took his breath away. Drágan stood on a beach wearing only board shorts and sunglasses. The makeup people must've put suntan oil on him because the perfection of his flat, elegantly defined muscles glistened in the sunlight. His long hair seemed to be flying to one side, as though in a breeze, and his face glowed.

"Wow."

"Hotter than hot, right?"

He nodded, feeling more inadequate than ever.

"So that one was taken earlier this year, for a summer catalogue," she went on. "Check out the next one I printed."

He slid the beach photo to the back of the stack and found himself looking at a shot of Drágan wearing what he assumed was supposed to be some modern dressy style for men, but to his eyes it just looked weird.

"Look at the date."

Isaac lowered his eyes to the bottom of the photo and gasped. "2010? The hell..." He met her gaze, the beginnings of fear creeping over him. "It can't be him."

"I know, right? Check out the rest."

Isaac slid that one to the back and barely glanced at what Drágan wore in the next. His eyes found the date scrawled in black sharpie: 2000. His breathing became ragged, and his heart pounded as he flipped through the pictures faster and faster. 1990, 1980, 1970, 1960, 1950, 1940, 1930, and the last, 1920. Lightheaded, he dropped into his chair, gripping the photos as though they held the secrets of the universe. He looked up and found Stephanie's lovely brown eyes regarding him with a similar look.

"They're not Photoshop or AI," she explained before he could ask. "I found lots more like these, but nothing before 1920. He's a popular model. With his looks, that's a 'duh.' "

"It's not possible," Isaac blurted, flipping through the photos again. The one from the 70s showed Drágan wearing long pants with flared bottoms and a flowery shirt. He studied it, and the others. The oldest ones from 1920 and 1930 were in black and white. He scrutinized every detail of the boy's face. It was Drágan, all right. "How?"

"Can you ask him," Stephanie replied casually, as though asking if Drágan would like to go on a date with her.

"Ask him if he's been alive more than a hundred years?" Isaac stared at her in amazement.

Apparently calmer than he felt, she shrugged.

"Why not? I mean, when I saw these pics, trust me, I freaked out. But, I've watched a lot of horror movies and read tons of books like you have and I've also done lots of research on legends and supposed monsters and, well, turns out they might be real. Some of them, anyway. And they don't have to be bad, right? I mean, Drágan hasn't hurt you or your mom yet, has he?"

"Yet?" Isaac considered the fears he'd already built up regarding Drágan and wondered if maybe he and his mom were wrong, that maybe Drágan was dangerous after all.

Stephanie's lovely face lit up. "Hey, maybe he's a vampire."

"You've seen him outside during the day," Isaac said, his mind suddenly whirling with possibilities, rather than fears.

"Maybe it's more like *The Picture of Dorian Gray,* you know, that book that's been made into a bunch of movies."

"Drágan's gorgeous enough for someone to make a painting that would keep him young forever."

Isaac put the photos on his desk. "Can I keep these to show him?"

"Sure."

"You won't tell anyone else, will you? Not even Mary Anne?"

Fellow cheerleader Mary Anne was Stephanie's best friend and they stuck to each other like glue.

"No, but you can fill me in tomorrow. He'll be there, right?"

"Yeah."

She glanced at a smart watch on her slim wrist. "I gotta go. My stepdad isn't at work today and he'd already started drinking before I left. I'm gonna kick it with Mary Anne. See you tomorrow." She started for the open door.

He was about to speak when she turned back. "I wasn't kidding, by the way. I'm really excited about your movie. I want to be a professional actress, so this is perfect."

She bounced from the room.

Excerpt from SPINNER

Excerpt from Book One in
The Healer Chronicles,
SPINNER

The following morning, Alex regarded himself in the bathroom mirror as he brushed his teeth. He'd showered and blow-dried his shoulder-length, choppy white-blond hair and it looked clean. People liked his blue eyes, when he didn't hide them behind his flowing bangs.

Alex finished pushing the brush up and down his teeth, and spat out the mint-flavored water, staring a moment at his soft, hairless cheeks and milky white skin. Sure, he seemed so innocent, a "sweet-faced boy," as his social workers had always described him to prospective foster parents. That's what made the whole thing worse. He did look like a nice kid. But no matter how hard he tried, he always screwed everything up. He always started spinning people. He couldn't help it. And once they figured out he was doing something weird, they got scared and wanted nothing more to do with him.

He'd already been through ten foster homes, and the only reason Jane kept him at this one was because she'd figured out what he could do.

"What are you?" he asked his reflection. As always, it didn't answer.

Jane Walters stood at the door with her ear pressed against it, while two boys sat at the kitchen table watching her.

Carlos, a burly high school junior, wolfed down his cereal, while freshman Juan glared with barely contained fury. Carlos grinned at the smaller boy. Juan flinched in fear and Carlos sniggered. Juan's cereal sat untouched in front of him as he reached with trembling fingers to touch his face, wincing at the pain. The left cheek and eye were black and blue and swelling rapidly.

A motorized sound came from behind the door, like a rising elevator.

Jane stepped away and jerked her thumb at Carlos. "You, out!"

Carlos's previous bravado with Juan dropped instantly. He swallowed his final mouthful and leapt from his chair. Snatching up a backpack from the floor, he bolted out the side door, never even glancing at Jane. She regarded the sullen Juan, folding her arms across her chest.

"You know what to do." Her tone left no room for argument.

"What if he don't wanna this time? He said he wouldn't no more."

"You know what'll happen to you if he won't," she snapped.

Juan nodded.

Jane observed her reflection in the large, ornately framed mirror, obviously looking pleased with what she saw.

She turned to him, practically pinning the petrified boy to his chair. "I'll be watching."

The motorized whirring s ground to a halt as Jane darted through the door into the hallway.

The door beside the rectangular dining table popped open and Alex rolled out in his wheelchair, wearing a Hawthorne Heights band shirt, black hoodie, skinny black jeans, his black and white high-top Converse shoes, and a backpack resting on his lap. He had Roy to thank for most of these clothes since Jane never spent a dime on him unless she had to.

He popped a small wheelie and shoved the door closed with a swipe of his hand, and then turned to Juan, whose head was bent toward his cereal bowl. Alex noted the behavior and frowned. It bothered him that he frightened Juan, but he didn't blame the kid. After all, he frightened almost everyone.

"Mornin', Juan," he offered in his most upbeat tone of voice as he dropped his backpack by the door. Was that upbeat? He so seldom felt that way he really didn't know what it sounded like.

"Hi, Alex."

Juan didn't look up. Alex noted the other bowl and half-filled glass of orange juice on the table and frowned.

"Carlos must 'a heard me comin' and bailed, huh?"

Juan said nothing.

Attempting to seem nonthreatening to the younger boy, Alex added, "Left his dishes this time. Jane'll be pissed."

Juan looked up, revealing his bruised face. "You mean 'Mom', right, Alex?"

Alex ignored the correction, gazing in shock at the other boy's battered face. Furious, he wheeled over to Juan. "Did she make Carlos—?"

Juan cut him off. "I fell, uh, hit the bed table. That's all."

He indicated the mirror on the wall with a slight head nod. Alex caught the movement and looked at Juan, blinking twice in response, his anger roiling.

Juan pleaded, "Alex, could you, you know…?"

His voice trailed off and he looked down at his cereal again. Alex scowled.

"I don't wanna go to school 'n look like this," Juan whispered, focusing his attention on the soggy corn flakes floating in his bowl like dead maggots.

Alex gazed long and hard at Juan. He was fourteen, but looked eleven or twelve, tiny and scrawny with brown skin, short hair, and big, fearful eyes. He wore baggy pants and baggy shirts, but they only highlighted how tiny he was. Had Alex ever seen the boy laugh or grin like a kid should? He didn't think so. But then, he didn't do those things either. How could they, living with a witch like Jane? He leaned in so Juan's head hid him from view of the mirror.

"You mean she don't want you to."

Juan's eyes looked round and filled with panic. "Please, Alex?"

"Aren't you afraid, like the other times?"

He reached out to touch Juan's bruised cheek, but Juan recoiled even before Alex's fingers reached him.

Alex felt that punch to the gut sensation each time someone flinched from him, which was almost everyone, except for Roy and the kids in his class.

"You are afraid. Guess I don' blame you."

Juan flushed red with embarrassment, turning his bruises a brighter shade of purple. "Alex, please?"

Alex sighed with resignation. His frown melted into a look of deep compassion as he brushed his bangs away from his eyes so Juan wouldn't be scared. At least, he didn't think he looked scary. The blue always seemed to calm people.

"Okay," Alex said, steeling himself for the pain to come. "Tell me."

Jane stood in a small closet directly behind the two-way mirror in the kitchen, smirking at the two men beside her. All the kids knew it was there, but they never knew when she might actually be on the other side. Another technique she'd developed to keep them in line. The men wore business suits, and one held a GoPro camera pointing through the glass at the two boys.

"Now watch real close," Jane admonished, though both men were already riveted to the drama playing out in the kitchen.

The younger of the two, Phil, watched intently, as though not surprised by what he was witnessing. As silver-haired Bob lifted the GoPro, his mouth dropped open in stunned disbelief.

Jane grinned as she turned from the boys to eye the two

men. Shocked by what he saw, Bob lowered the camera and watched with his own eyes.

"You idiot, keep filming!" Jane snapped, her voice like a firecracker. Bob recovered from the initial surprise and whipped the camera up, continuing to record.

Phil's expression remained unreadable to Jane, but she didn't care.

These men were flunkies. The moneyman was all that mattered.

"Wish we had audio," Phil muttered.

"You'll get it from the other camera," Jane said, directing his attention to the cupboard behind the boys. The door was ajar. From this angle, through the two-way glass, she saw the blinking red light as it recorded.

Phil nodded while Jane watched, grinning at the stunned expressions of the two men beside her.

Through the mirror, she observed Alex spin his black magic, saw the pained expression on his face, and grinned when Juan, now uninjured, stared in wide-eyed fear at the freak beside him.

Yes, you're a freak, Alex, she thought, *but you're a freak who's going to make me rich.*

Alex's eyes remained closed, his features intent as his bruised face returned to normal. Several moments passed before his eyes fluttered open. "Man, Carlos—I mean that table—really hit you hard."

Juan had pulled away from Alex as far as his chair would

allow. His eyes were wide and anxious, and his voice quavered. "Yeah. Well, I... uh, thanks."

He looked down at the table again, obviously afraid to meet Alex's gaze. Alex watched him sadly, and then glanced at the mirror. He scowled at his own reflection.

She was there, probably wearing that evil smile she had. Fighting down the temptation to flip his middle finger at her, Alex turned to Juan.

"C'mon," he said with a heavy sigh. "We gonna be late for school."

He smiled as best he could manage, and Juan nodded. He rose from his chair and snatched his ratty backpack from the floor at his feet. Alex grabbed his own pack and rolled to the door, pulling it open. Juan skirted past him, making Alex feel like he had a horrible disease or something. He'd just helped the boy—for the seventh time already—and Juan was still afraid of him. But Juan's reaction was typical. Unless he spun them afterwards, everyone who saw what he could do pretty much freaked. He rolled outside and yanked the door shut behind him.

Inside the closet, Jane turned to Bob, who continued to run the GoPro even though the kitchen was empty.

"You can stop recording now," she said, folding her arms across her chest.

Bob suddenly realized there was nothing left to film and shut off the camera, staring at Jane with amazement. His face was ashen, as though he'd seen a ghost. Phil's eyes glittered with excitement, which Jane interpreted as astonishment at what he'd just seen.

"A million, remember," she insisted. "You tell him. Not a penny less."

Bob wiped his sweaty palms against his gray dress pants. "Oh, we'll definitely tell him, Ms. Walters. You can count on that."

Jane grinned.

Excerpt from I KNOW WHEN YOU'RE GOING TO DIE

Excerpt from Book One in
The Film Milieu Thriller Series,
I KNOW WHEN YOU'RE GOING TO DIE

I toss and turn all night, images of the old man's craggy face and piercing gaze filling my dreams. Each time I wake, I hear his scratchy voice repeating the same words over and over again: "I gave you a great gift, boy. Or maybe a curse."

What does that mean?

The next day, when J.C. accompanies me to the mission, he's dressed in designer jeans and a fancy shirt fit for a dance club. Maybe that's why, before we're even finished serving lunch, everyone clamors for him to perform. He's been dancing since he was little and knows so many styles I can't keep track. Dancing and fashion are the loves of his life. He cranks hip hop on his phone and launches into an awesome routine that includes some cool break dance moves, his ebony hair doing its own dance against his forehead as he spins. Everyone is clapping and cheering within minutes.

As I ladle soup into chipped white bowls and pass out fresh rolls, I keep thinking of Mr. Franklin, the old man who died. Everything about that encounter troubles me and I find my mind wandering from J.C.'s performance. To the regular mission staff, death is a common occurrence, almost a daily one. Even I've seen people die down here, but this time was different. Especially the way I felt when I locked eyes with him.

"Make wise choices."

My thoughts are interrupted by raucous applause. The song —most likely from one of those Step Up movies J.C. adores— ends and my best friend stops dancing. Staff, volunteers, and homeless alike shout and clap with gusto.

Sweat beading his forehead, J.C. looks over at me and grins. I grin back and toss him a thumbs up.

After lunch, we head to a nearby McDonald's and buy bags of hamburgers, chicken sandwiches, and fries to give out on the streets. I make momentary eye contact with each person I hand a bag to because I want them to know they're human like me. But I can't hold it for more than a second until, beneath the dim shade of the freeway overpass on Main Street, this one man grasps my arm as he takes his bag. He's a regular named Hank, an older guy with a limp who always wears a dirty Dodgers cap and mismatched clothes I'm sure he found in a dumpster.

"Thank you, Leo." Hank's voice is strained, but sincere.

I force myself to look into his grateful eyes and our gazes lock. I can't seem to look away. It's like I'm being drawn into Hank's very soul. Then I see it! Gasping, I lurch back and yank my arm away from him.

He recoils, looking stung by my action, and I want to apologize, but no words come. I'm paralyzed by what I just saw and can only offer him a silent nod.

Gripping the bag with gnarled fingers, Hank lurches down Main Street until he reaches the corner and turns out of sight.

J.C. steps around in front of me. "Hey, Leo, you okay? You look like you saw a ghost."

"I know... when he's... going to... die." I barely get the words out.

J.C. stares at me. "Huh?"

I shiver, my hand still outstretched from giving Hank the Big Mac and fries. I look down at it—my fingers are trembling. I pull them into a fist and lower my arm to my side.

"Leo?"

I face J.C., but don't meet his gaze, a chill enveloping my body and causing me to break into a cold sweat. "I-I never look people in the eye, J.C. You- you know that, right?"

He tilts his head like I'm crazy. "Duh! What are you talking about, man?" I glance again at the corner where Hank vanished. Homeless people lie on blankets and tarps or on the bare gray sidewalks. Others lounge beside colorful nylon tents or shelters made from cardboard boxes. I know many of these people by name and they know me. Several of the women stare at me with concern. I must look as scared as I feel.

"Yo, Leo, anybody home in there?"

I turn back to J.C. but focus on the lower half of his face. His brow is drawn together, and his mouth is clamped in a straight line. It's a worried look.

I clear my throat. "I looked into Hank's eyes when I handed him the food."

J.C. punches me on the shoulder and grins. "Awesome. That's progress, right?"

I shiver again. Traffic noise and passing cars distract me for a moment and derail my train of thought. I stare at the dimple in the center of J.C.'s chin and whisper, "I saw him dead, J.C."

His mouth drops open. "Huh?"

I shake my head, those horrific images fixed to the backs of my retinas like photographs. "He-he was all bloody and kind of twisted up. I-I couldn't see how he died, but I knew when he died."

He gives me one of his hard looks and then bursts out laughing. "Good one, bro. You had me going there for a sec."

"I'm not joking, J.C. He's about to die!"

I start jogging down Main, but soon I'm running, ignoring the dust I kick up from the sidewalk as I hurry in the direction Hank took. I hear J.C. curse under his breath and then his footsteps as he follows. The homeless ladies touch my shoulder in gratitude as I pass and offer their best, mostly toothless, smiles. I'm too spooked by what I've just seen to return anything but a quick nod.

"Leo, wait up."

I don't slow my stride and feel, rather than see, J.C.'s loping gait alongside me.

As I stop at the corner of Main and one of its busy cross streets, a screech of tires, followed by a loud thud and cry of human anguish, pierces my ears. I break into a sprint.

A crowd is already gathering in front of Marguerite's Place, a Mexican restaurant where I sometimes buy food for people on the streets. Traffic at the intersection has momentarily halted and people clamber out of their cars for a better look. I run to the edge of the crowd and muscle my way through.

A man's voice laments, "The light was green. He just stepped out in front of me!"

My heart rate quickens. A large pickup truck, its bed laden with gardening equipment, has stopped mid-turn onto Main, a line of cars halted behind it. A body lies in the crosswalk. Sirens assail my ears.

"Hey, kid, watch out!" a man says as I push my way past an inside ring of onlookers. I hear J.C toss out a couple of curse words in Spanish and another voice responding, "Puta madre."

I inch my way closer to the pickup so I can get a clear view of the body. I immediately recognize the ragged jeans and baggy flannel shirt. My heart pounds and I can scarcely breathe.

"Leo, what are you—"

J.C. stops in midsentence, and I feel his arm brush up against me, but I don't glance over. My gaze is fixed on Hank's bloody face. The McDonald's bag must've flown from his hand onto Main Street because it's already been crushed by a passing car. Blotches of ketchup adorn the pavement and mingle with the blood pooling from the back of Hank's head. The ratty blue Dodger's cap is splashed with ghastly streaks of red.

"Holy crap," J.C. whispers beside me. "You were right!"

My head feels light. The heat rising from the hot asphalt nearly overcomes me. I foresaw this man's death! My knees grow weak, and I grab J.C. by the arm. He wraps his arm around me, gripping my shoulder so I don't collapse. The wail of sirens gets louder.

J.C. leans into my ear, "Come on, Leo. We should jet."

I stare numbly at Hank's dead gaze and twisted limbs. I feel J.C. dragging me back and finally turn to follow him.

We escape the scene just as the police arrive and hurry back to my car, which is parked blocks away in front of the old Hotel Cecil on Main. Unlike all the other kids at La Costa High who have fancy cars, I drive a three-year- old Prius that has visible parking lot dings on the sides and "only" cloth upholstery, all of which embarrasses my mother like you wouldn't believe.

I feel J.C. slip his hand into the side pocket of my baggy cargo pants to pull out my key fob. He opens the door and eases me into the passenger seat.

"Wait," I mumble. "I'm driving."

J.C. shakes his head. "Not spooked as hell like you are. I'll drive." I nod absently and he sprints around to the driver's side.

He knows me well enough to know I don't want to talk about what happened. Not right now, anyway. We leave downtown L.A. behind us and head back via freeway and palm-lined streets to our beachfront town of La Costa in a heavy silence. He doesn't even crank the mariachi music like he usually does, for which I'm grateful.

www.ingramcontent.com/pod-product-compliance
Lightning Source LLC
LaVergne TN
LVHW090055190325
806178LV00001B/61